SOLITUDE IS A VICE, TOO

A Novel

Orlando A. Rebolledo

Amazon Publishing

ISBN-13: 9798499317167
ISBN-10: 1477123456

Cover design by: Art Painter
Library of Congress Control Number: 2018675309
Printed in the United States of America

Para Abuela Rin... and for me.

CONTENTS

CHAPTER 1

You found yourself tossing on your bed.

You float around the room; you smell the stench to which your time in the room has inured you, and I lean closer to your face.

I notice a grimace on your eyes, the frown you rarely dare muster on your brow: the sadness you've contained but know you deserve.

Your eyes are open. And in their dark reflection flash the various aphorisms you keep reading to yourself.

The Stoics.

You love the idea of being one.

A writer. A poet. A dramatist!

You revere the possibility of becoming a glimmer of what Seneca has grown to be inside your heart.

I see you finally get off the bed, walk to the bathroom, and urinate what waste you had accrued throughout the night.

Your eyes closed.

Your attention struck.

I find you cross-legged on the toilet trying to meditate, and wonder: *shouldn't you do that somewhere else?*

But perhaps you crave discomfort.

Perhaps you've conjured up a storm inside yourself and you're glad to have a motive for which to pine, to cry, to milk misery's teat and 'match your inspiration with its language.'

You're hoarding pain.

And I get to live in it.

But why would you care?

After all, we've barely met, or truth be told: you've just

now heard of me.

I am your *daemon*, Orlando.

Call it conscience, or spirit, or soul, or the voice inside your head. Regardless, it's about time we know each other.

It's about time you see beyond the silver spoon and learn of the calloused hands that held it.

CHAPTER 2

The reasons don't matter, but you found yourself recused to a hotel room for an indefinite time.

Food was brought to you at the door. And you weren't allowed to leave.

But it did allot you time to think of all the hurt you had caused and all the hurt you now suffered as what you fancied 'karmic deliverance.'

You journaled.

You meditated.

You wrote yourself cathartic letters of 'self-impalement.' And you ate lots of food that, though unappetizing, was free, and you didn't get 'fat.'

You thought of what Blaise Pascal wrote in 1654 about how "all of humanity's problems stem from man's inability to sit quietly in a room alone," and wondered if the whole idea was an oxymoron.

Is 'man' unable because there is no such thing as 'quiet' for a human mind? Why even add the word 'alone'? Would 'man' be able to sit quietly in a room *accompanied*? Is being alone what prompts the 'inability'? Do we have to be seated? Or, *am I focusing on stupid shit to sound smart?*

Shit.

You thought of a colleague onboard a ship who thought curse words were an unnecessary obscenity, and you were out for a walk when it occurred to you just how powerful a timely obscenity can be.

Words are meant to portray feelings, you thought. *And every utterance of* fuck *is laden with so much otherwise inexpressible pas-*

*sion, and results in such a swift, mono-syllabic release that, well...
it's sheer linguistic beauty!*

Whenever a high-ended thought would populate your mind, or whenever you found yourself looped in a whirlpool of esoteric trash: a simple *fuck,* or *shit,* thrown into a messy sentence would wrench you off your dark reveries.

To deny the latent power of a curse word is to refuse of language its most effective form of release.

And, *fuck that!*

CHAPTER 3

"Tell me about your grandmother," I said. "You said she sent you videos telling you about her childhood."

"Yes," you said, "my grandmother from my mother's side. My father's mother died some years ago. We weren't close."

"What does it matter if you were close?"

"I figured you'd ask me to tell you her story as well, but I don't know it. I never asked."

"Because you weren't close..."

"Right."

"So you've always known your other grandma's story, then?"

"No. I've only heard it recently. I drove her to the mall last year and I asked her to tell me about her childhood."

"I see."

"What do you see?"

"If your father's mother had been alive today, would you have asked her about her childhood?"

"Yes, I would've."

"Even if, as you say, you weren't close?"

"That wouldn't have mattered. I would've asked."

"Right. It doesn't matter."

"What are you saying?"

"I'm saying you didn't ask her because you didn't care. And the only reason you know this grandma's story is because she lived long enough to see you start to care. I'm saying that you can't lie to me. I'm your *daemon*. It'd be easier to lie to yourself than to me. Pretense is pointless between us. You don't know her story because she died before you gave a shit, not because you weren't close."

Daemon.

Yes. The word must've popped out and it was mentioned casually, but it was about time I introduced myself to you.

You were surprised to hear it, and for a time thought yourself mad, but you soon assimilated.

You dubbed me: Logos.

CHAPTER 4

The Stoics believed in an immanent deity, meaning instead of a transcendental god (existing outside of our universe and looking over us) the Stoic god *was* the universe, an all-pervading agent of reason and creation – the *logos* - from whom each person had a portion.

And this portion, this gift of reason particular to the individual which tethers you to the universe and its divinity, is the *daemon.* It could be said, then, as your *daemon*, that I am also the *logos* living within you, granting you an engine for beauty, imagination, and raucous thought.

This dynamic between people and divinity is referenced in almost every system of faith and thought. In Christianity, for example, the *daemon* is called the 'the guardian angel,' vying for your safety, happiness, and piousness with the express purpose of 'shepherding' you into heaven.

But!

Enough on theology, cosmology, and metaphysics.

This is a different story.

CHAPTER 5

"I want to fictionalize the story," you said, "heavily."

"Why?"

"I don't want anyone to know what's real and what is not," you said, "and I'm worried she won't like her life exposed like that."

"Why don't you start and see where it goes?"

"I don't know where to start."

"Start where she started."

"Easy to say..."

"Easy to be afraid before you start to write."

"I'm starting now."

CHAPTER 6

She didn't know her full name until the first grade. It was 1950. Everyone called her Rin, pronounced Reen.

She learned her full name in school, being taught to write it on a green sheet of construction paper, and not only did she learn her name was an entirely different thing from what she responded to, but that she had a middle name – which implied there was at least one more name after it – and a surname (two, in fact: her father's and her mother's, as is customary in Panama).

She remembers this moment, as she puts it, "as my first identity crisis."

"The entire collection of scribbles," she said, "– vowels and consonants with accents and capital letters – was like several claims of ownership. My first name meant I cried at birth and so by expressing some form of discontent, I laid claim to life. My middle name was given by way of reinforcement to my first one, like an adjective, in a way, to color in whatever doubt there was in my having an identity; but, the curious thing, was when the surnames began to show: the first one to ascribe me to my father, as was custom, and the second to acknowledge my mother's credit in the matter."

Growing up she had been a sweet girl. Not to say she didn't carry on to be a sweet lady, but she'd become selective with her sweetness. As a child, all cheer and buoyant giggles, this sweetness played in her like a concert: all were welcome to take it in. But as life carried her on to see and categorize her interactions, she made a guest list to her concerts. Not to say she was nasty to the uninvited, not at all - she was always courteous - Rin thought courtesy is every person's right, but respect – "there's a differ-ence!" – must be earned.

Her earliest memory can be traced back to her mother's death, of which she remembers nothing but the aftermath: when her father brought a new woman to grace his bed. Rin had a sister and two brothers, whose names we shall keep anonym-ous for their existence is merely acknowledged by way of fur-nishing a clause, and of whom we don't hear much about until their death. Even then, they were of no particular import.

She lived in a small house over a hill.

"The countryside was much quieter, then," she told you, "electric lights were not a thing and even candles were a luxury. When the day was done, we were also done."

She smiled a little when she spoke, and you weren't sure if it was because the memories were happy or because she was happy they were memories. She was here now. Not a vulnerable girl anymore, but grown and strong. She was loved now.

She calls you *lijo*, which is a contraction of *el hijo*: the son.
She began.

CHAPTER 7

The woman was tall, but it could be my memory is distorted.

We always think our monsters to be giants.

But she was beautiful.

Yes, *lijo*, she was stunning in a way the dim-lit room couldn't keep in the shadows. The door was still open and my sister and I were picking up rocks from the dirt floor inside the house. It hurts when you step barefoot on little rocks, especially if they're the pointy kind. The round ones sink nicely where the dirt is deep, and even if you step on them they slide between your toes and you find them later sleeping with you in bed. Not so bad.

"*Hola, mijitas,*" she said addressing only us. My brothers, I supposed, were off-limits to her malice, them being boys and sole concern of my father. "We'll get along fine."

She didn't say she hoped we'd get along. She stated it. Declared it before anything else was said. She announced what she expected us to do when Daddy was around. Get along. Fine, indeed.

And I know the tale of evil stepmothers is as old as time and this cliché, but I never promised you my story was unique. Perhaps the world would be much better if it were unique, but it's the only one I've got.

CHAPTER 8

Before we go on about your grandmother, perhaps we should talk about your mother.

The US invasion of Panama 'officially' took place between December 20th, 1989, and the end of January in 1990. Manuel Antonio Noriega had been Panama's *de facto* leader, general, and dictator until Operation Just Cause knocked him off his tyrannous throne. The city was mayhem. People would go missing overnight, and the few times they were found you couldn't tell if they were human or rotten road-kill. Fortunately, *El Cara De Piña*'s despotic reign was taken down with the turn of the decade.

It wouldn't be a year until you were born. Meanwhile, your mother was out looting chicken feet from a supermarket, and your father was on a ship smuggling jeans from Mexico into Cuba. You were a chance implosion never meant to explode, which in the end did neither. You combusted.

Your mother grew up in the country, which is the extent of what you know of her childhood because you've never asked. What you know of her early years can be mustered in that single story where she ran away from your grandmother's *atajona:* a thin stick used to goad horses into running and apparently to scare misbehaving children. It's called a riding crop in English, but what chased her was more rudimentary, and painful.

She'd tell of how she climbed up a tree and jumped from branch to branch like your average skilled monkey, and you thought about how your youthful infatuation with *parkour* could've been inherited from her, but you never mentioned it.

Whenever you'd hide from her or not introduce her to your friends in school she'd feel insulted, thinking you were embarrassed by her when truly you were worried she'd belittle you in front of your friends, as she did when you were at home. In these cases, she would tell you of when your grandfather went to pick her up in school smelling of cow manure and how she didn't feel embarrassed, how she felt proud her father had a job and at least, as opposed to many other fathers, showed up.

And even though she had it all wrong about your embarrassment, you never denied her assumption. In your young brain, you thought you were better off letting her think you were embarrassed than telling her you were afraid. You didn't know – and how could you? – that she'd sooner be a monster than not enough for you.

How better off you could both have been if you had spoken to each other. But that wasn't the way, at least not in your family. Repression, lies, and the occasional wrathful outburst was the actual norm. And that was that.

The car rides to school were some of the worst situations you remember with her. There was nowhere you could go. Luckily your sister liked sitting in the front, so you sat in the back diagonally from your mother, far from what you had calculated was her arm's reach. She could not hit you, even if you did dare open your mouth to speak. At first, you couldn't figure what it was she wanted to hear, and when you did you couldn't bring yourself to say it. You knew she'd smell the bullshit in your tone. The best thing to do, you realized, was to be quiet. And you were, for years, right up until you moved out.

You grew up to be clingy, because though they showered you with acts of service, they recriminated and threw them in your face, which instead of making you feel loved, it made you feel guilty; it made you feel like you were a burden, a nuisance, that they were stuck with you and you were nothing but a leech and they wanted out but still stayed and so you should be grateful and submissive.

This led to insecurity.

This led to you demanding from all of your relationships constant gestures of affection, constant proof that it wasn't a nuisance to love you, which in turn did make it a nuisance. It made you jealous and accusatory, always suspicious of why and how somebody could ever love you.

It made you hate yourself.

CHAPTER 9

"How many days have passed?" I asked you.

"I'm not sure," you said, "I haven't checked."

"Why?"

"I forgot."

"You forgot or you want to forget?"

"Why would I want to forget?"

"I don't know."

"But you *do* know."

"Yes, but *you* should know. Not me."

"But," you rolled your eyes, "*you* know it already."

"You know it's not a *daemon's* job to hand you realizations. You should make them on your own."

"Then what *is* your job?"

"Well, a *daemon's* job would be to assist in your inspiration, propel your industry, validate your discipline and, on occasion, if you've earned it, link you to the Collective Soul from which I could feed you with the lofty thoughts and beautiful musings of old and new. You'd be embodied by the world itself, as your soul begins to 'match its higher inspiration with its language,' as Seneca said."

"Again with Seneca?"

"Dude knew his shit," I said to you, "and what shit he didn't know he dressed in gorgeous metaphor."

"Well, I need to get up and work," you said to me, but mostly to yourself, "otherwise I'll wallow in here until the food comes."

"Get to it then," I said, leaning over your shoulder as you sat in front of the computer. "You were writing about when your grandmother first met her stepmother, Claudia."

"Right."

* * *

In the videos, your grandmother sat on a couch where generations of you have slept, watched TV, and heard her read stories from the Bible.

The couch is maroon with large, pink flowers on the cushions. It's still comfortable, despite being at least five decades. Perhaps because of it. And it may not sound like time enough for three generations, but it has been.

The first one to sleep on it must've been her, waiting the long hours of the night, waiting for the steps of a man who rarely walked toward her, for the sound of a door that never opened when he went out drinking with his friends.

Perhaps the second one to sleep on it was your grandfather, whenever she'd finally give up and lock herself in the room, refusing to share her bed with someone who wouldn't even share his time.

If we disregard any guests who may have slept on the couch over years, we would be right to say your aunt was the third person to sleep on it. Then it was your uncle. She often had people over, too, and perhaps it was there she knit her first straw hat. Perhaps it was there she thought to sew first *pollera*. And perhaps it was there, in 1967, where your grandmother sat late one afternoon listening to the radio, waiting for it to say she could get on a horse and ride two hours to the hospital postpartum and pick up her newborn.

Your mother, born so wild her lungs couldn't hold the storm she had inside, was born with asphyxia. But it was time. She felt better now, she learned to pace herself, her breathing steadied, and she wanted mommy.

CHAPTER 10

The first few days Claudia was passive.

She was taking her bearings of the house, the workers, the neighbors, and particularly my father's affinity to us. We cleaned, brought wood for the fire, hauled water from the river, gathered fruit, and tended to the chickens.

Claudia spent her days walking around the village. Her knees were always red and dirty. She came home shouting for water, food, and for both of us to massage her feet, do her nails, and clean her knees. My father came home at night, and we were excited to see him because he'd always have glitter on his face. We would dab his face with our fingers and then put the glitter on our faces. Then he'd go inside the house.

We prayed before every meal and ate our dinner quietly. I once asked my father about God. He said God was the creator of the world, but he didn't go beyond that. I asked Claudia once if God had made other worlds, and she said, "No, because where would it go? If there were another world it would imply there is a bigger space than our world that can hold this world and the other one, and that's blasphemy."

As ignorant as she was, her reasoning went deeper than she knew. It's terrifying when you don't know if you should fear a monster's mind more than its claws. There's a level of comfort and hope when you think you can at least outsmart the beast. The claws are scary, but they're simple. If they don't touch you then you're fine. But there is little we can do when there's a monstrous brain to top her off. A monster's ideas are more insidious than its claws. And her first idea was also the worst. I know this because it was also the last. She wanted us to leave.

I was ten.

The boys were of use to the farm, and as far as the housework went it'd be easy for her to take over. Her family lived nearby, and whatever help she needed she could get from them. She wanted children of her own, and if my father was supporting two daughters on top of his beloved sons it wouldn't be feasible to support any more children. And she couldn't have that.

We had to go.

Neither of us was there for the deliberations, if there were even any, but we found out at night before dinner: when all the work was done, and no meal was wasted on us.

"You'll be moving with your uncle down the river," my father said. "They're outside to pick you up."

I didn't even ask them why. I was certainly confused, but not entirely surprised. A worn, saggy backpack hung from the handle of the door. She packed it for us, which was surprising because I would've expected her to make us pack it ourselves. Still, it couldn't have taken her long. I remember noticing how everything two little girls owned could fit in a small backpack, how it almost weighed nothing because it was mostly dust and air.

I had never met my uncle, let alone his wife.

My aunt took a quick look at us and said, "They will do."

We both got on one horse and followed theirs.

The first couple of minutes were silent.

It was dark already.

"Auntie," I called out, "we didn't eat dinner."

They looked at each other, and I could swear I heard a sigh, though it could've been the breeze.

"We already ate," she said.

CHAPTER 11

Your grandfather doesn't know how old he is.

Your father's father.

He was brought to Panama from Colombia by his godmother, whose name, coincidentally, was also Claudia. To have a representative of good and evil bearing the same name, in the same family, is coincidence enough to make anyone believe in fate. But not us.

We shall call it a coincidence that two women with the same name played pivotal roles in the lives of two of your grandparents – one constructive, one destructive – which are in the end pivotal roles toward your formation as a thing who eventually existed. And I.

Good Claudia wasn't a blood relative, but she was your grandfather's mother. Your great grandmother. She raised him by herself on the Atlantic coast, where he learned how to swim, fell in love with fishing, and taught himself calligraphy.

Your grandfather is of Italian descent, has as much hair as he does skin, and is often so polite he's rude. You'd witness this oxymoron in his demeanor toward your mother, of whom he never approved, and you'd later find yourself emulating it in the workplace. It shows decorum and power at the same time. It works.

Your father has always resented how your grandfather overtly favors your aunt, the middle child, over his other two children. He often tells the story of how your grandfather had a fishing boat he named after her, and how when it sank, he bought another one and also named it after her. You could tell it bothered him, but you later learned that in those days it was customary for boats to be named after women, not men.

He didn't name the second boat after his second daughter because it would imply his first daughter had died. And he couldn't bear the thought even if indirectly through the sinking of a boat.

Still, all the little boy understood, and remembers, is rejection.

Little acts like these, inexcusably unconscious, of which nobody is at fault, are easily branded into a young boy's mind, festering through puberty and adulthood. The feeling of rejection stains all subsequent emotions, promotes itself from incidence to denominator, and becomes a founding principle of character. Worse yet, if left unexamined, the feeling will reproduce itself, repeat itself, and make its inevitable migration onto the next generation.

And here you are.

***

"Will you include your mother and father in the novel?" I asked you.

"No."

"Why?"

"The story is about my grandmother," he said, "I want to focus it on her."

"You're worried she'll die before you finish it?"

"What? I –"

"You are. You know I only ask you so that you say things out loud, but as your *daemon*, I know."

"I know! I get it! And yes, I obviously want it published before she dies."

"You know writing it in Spanish would speed things up. She'd be able to read it, too."

"The time it would take me to become as proficient in Spanish as I am in English would outweigh the time it would take for the book to be translated."

"Then she'd be reading a translated version of your words."

"I've added and taken a lot," you said. "It's fiction by now."

"Why?"

"So she keeps her privacy."

"You're worried she'll feel invaded."

"Yes."

"You think the book will be famous?"

"If I don't believe in it, who will?"

"Are you worried someone will sue you?"

"That's a factor."

"Shouldn't be."

"Can we get back to work?"

"Sure."

"What should we do next?"

"Maybe something about your own life?"

"I want to be a novelist, not a memoirist."

"You should start by being a writer."

"Am I not writing?"

"No."

"Then what am I doing?"

"Typing words."

"That makes me a writer."

"Not until you finish a project."

"You mean getting published is the only thing that makes me a writer?"

"No. I'm saying having written something, to completion, is what makes you a writer."

"I don't agree."

"You're all over the place, starting projects and leaving them and starting other ones and you never finish anything. You've made many things, and yet you've created nothing."

"Isn't that part of the process?"

"No. Remember what Neil Gaiman said?"

"No."

"You do, technically, through me. You just can't recall it."

"Are you going to tell me?"

"'You learn more from finishing a failure than from starting a success.'"

***

The reason I ask you to write about your life is that many parts of it affect the way you see the world, your reactions, the preconceptions you have of people and situations. Your self-esteem. I bet you can barely remember the first time you had a drink.

At first, you made a point of being the only one in high school who did not drink. You took pride in showing off that bit of social rebellion and, as your success rate in nightclubs showed, you did well without the boost in confidence.

And then: the girl.

The girl you thought you loved but it really was infatuation.

You were roughly sixteen years old, two years younger than Panama's legal drinking age, and though most of your classmates were already drinking at parties, you were yet to give in to the poison. I can't particularly recall why it is that you didn't want to drink back then. You use to say it was because you were afraid of letting your brain take control, that you were terrified of being left inside your mind as you saw yourself possessed by someone else. A spectator to your life.

Essentially, you were afraid of me.

You didn't know of me back then but you were oddly aware of another consciousness tethered to your own. This, perhaps, as far as I can surmise, is how our one-of-a-kind relationship came to be. You see, a *daemon* and a human shouldn't be able to communicate the way we do. But you don't care about that, you don't want to be unique at the cosmic level, you want to matter here, in your spectrum, on Earth.

You finally gave in during Carnival, a yearly festival celebrated in Panama sometime between February and March. The festival itself dates back to Venice in the 1400s, where the celebration of debauchery, sexuality, desire, and the indulging of all conceivable pleasures were given leeway before the period of Lent began.

The word is said to come from the Late Latin *carne levare,* or even *carne vale,* which roughly translates to 'farewell to meat' or a 'removal of meat.' Some interpretations suggest, instead, that *carne* translates to 'flesh,' meaning the renouncement of pleasures before the conclusion of the festival in Ash Wednesday.

Carnival is celebrated in many countries where Western Christianity is predominant. The largest Carnival celebration, by far, according to the Guinness World Records, is held in Rio de Janeiro, Brazil. But the festival is held all over.

In France, for instance, the day before Ash Wednesday was a day where people would engorge themselves and eat as much as they could. They called it Fat Tuesday and brought it to their American colonies where it's now famously called, in French: *Mardi Gras.*

Carnival, carnaval, carnevale, or whatever other variation you may know it by, means liberty of expression. People rejoice in the opportunity to revel in the rejection of regular societal norms: boundaries made dim, lust uninhibited, language unrestricted, nudity socially accepted, and the overall mockery of custom, decency, and propriety is rapturously embraced. Costumes are worn in bombastic fashion: personal expression, eccentricity, peculiarities, the satirical parading of genitalia – anything of everything! – is condoned.

It's curious to me that while in Panama homophobia, transphobia, biphobia, and any other kind of identity-based phobia is still rampant, even more back then, for those few days of Carnival a man could dress in drag and dance to his heart's content wearing a million colors and only suffer a thousand frowns instead of the usual million. All this before Lent: Profligacy right up to Submission.

Every year you and your family would go to a small town in the countryside, Ocu, where as far as we can remember you had rejoiced in the simplicity of living in a small town, jovial, and best of all: where your parents were so busy and entertained they didn't have time for you. This meant not being grounded, no shouting, no insults, and a far-ranging leash with which to live.

Even now, you remember the little freedoms you used to take.

You would go places without telling them and come back without them asking where you'd been. And it wasn't anything adventurous or promiscuous. No. Freedom for you was as simple as riding a bike to the nearest convenience store, buying yourself a *Kist* apple soda, and drinking it in the parking lot.

There were many snacks you included in your freedom-runs: tamarind balls coated in sugar, *Nucita* packets, *salaitos* (dried, salted plums), *mafas* (braided super-fried dough), yuquitas (fried cassava chips), *Kachitos*, *chicharron* (fried pork rinds), and a Colombian bag of chips called *El Golpe* from which you exclusively ate the bacon bits.

Panamanian convenience stores are more like what in New York is known as a *bodega,* which is Spanish for cellar or depot, than a 7-Eleven, Lawson's, or ABC Store. They are almost invariably owned by Chinese immigrants, and so kids called the stores 'el chino.'

The day started with a round of firecrackers.

You'd come down the stairs to the kitchen and find everyone obsessing over a bag of hot bread fresh off the local bakery. The thing was flavorless and dry, thought it was indeed warm, but you never understood the hype. Every day they were as excited as the day before, and the bread never tasted any better. What you *were* excited about was the *sao.* Boiled pig feet and ham hocks marinated in a mixture of vinegar, cucumbers, onions, lemon juice, and a touch of *aji chombo.* Panamanian *sao* originated from Colon, on the Atlantic side, where your father and grandfather had grown up. The word most likely comes from the English word 'sow,' and it's a delicious, fatty, popularly nasty delight.

The house had three stories. The first floor had a kitchen, two bathrooms, and two showers. The facilities inside the house were for the women and the ones outside for the men. The older adults slept on the second floor: your uncle, who owned the house, your parents, and other people over forty and their children. The third floor was the 'cool' floor. All your cousins and their friends slept there.

You slept on the second floor with your parents.

After breakfast, everyone would pack up the coolers with beers, liquor, spirits, mixers, ice, and whatever trinkets each of us would use at the festivities. Every day you'd follow a different route around town. People would offer up their houses to host our particular portion of the festival, which was divided into *Calle Arriba, Calle Abajo,* and *Calle* Centro due to their vicinity to a river you never saw. You were part of *Calle Centro.*

You went from party-house to party-house in the vein of the Via Crucis fourteen Stations of the Cross. Each house hosted a conglomeration of folkloric dances, live music, traditional foods, and a cistern truck shooting water at the drunk, dancing crowd singing along to the yearly Carnival Jingle.

You used to wander around these places looking at the different gatherings of people and finding nothing of yourself in any of them, but it was fun to pop in and out of every single group and at the end of the day having experienced all of them. You remember thinking you were the only one who did this, seeing how nobody ever left their cliques and never experienced the whole as you did.

But you were wrong.

All you did was isolate yourself as you always did and then complain about your lot and how there was nothing to do about it.

Culecos. Murgas. The ever-catchy *Morena Sirena* song you'd hear at least twice every hour. All these words with their imbedded memories now trickle from your past as you sit in bed, locked up, the silence on your tongue paining like a phantom limb because, Orlando, back then you resented their society for your tongue's mutilation, but it was your insecurities which did the amputation.

You *chose* to say nothing.

You ask me what you could've done back then and I tell you there wasn't much and this is true. You were but a child. Overrated and underrated by the same people you were trying to impress. But you're learning now. Slowly, the more we speak to each other the more you realize that past a certain age your traumas are your own – you cannot blame your parents anymore – but syour triumphs are yours as well!

Your demise came during Fat Tuesday, *Martes de Carnaval,* and you must've consumed half a bottle of rum on your own to show this girl that you could drink, even if you had never drunk before, even if, to your dismay, there was not a single thing you could do to impress her because she wasn't into you. Still, you imbibed your libations and got as inebriated as the most preposterous of the thousand wretches wandering about the town.

Later on, when it was time to relax by the front porch – your parents were partying elsewhere – you felt the need to puke.

You had no water and no food in your stomach.

How could you have thought of nourishment, after all, when the only thing you'd think to feed on was her attention?

What you liked about her was her freedom. She spoke her mind, did what she wanted: she drank, smoked. She lived loudly. Meanwhile, you had always been kept on a leash: not drinking, not smoking, and certainly not speaking your mind – though this you mostly did to yourself – and, if we're honest, had they not disavowed the other stuff, it would've turned out badly for you.

You don't handle vice well. A drop of debauchery has always been enough to break you. Your parent's methods were ill-advised but they weren't wrong. There may be no addiction in your character, but we both know there is ample room for obsession. You squeeze as much as you can out of something from fear of it being taken away.

Yet another childhood trauma…

Every time you got a new toy or were excited about something, they'd hold it over your head threatening to take it away for the even slightest of reasons. But you're an adult now, man. Past a certain age, every trauma is on you.

You either feed it, or you starve it.

It's your choice.

Your father was the first to notice you were drunk. It was easy enough to tell: you were speaking, smiling, laughing, even with everyone around, and for a brief moment your father was happy to see you socializing, fitting in – finally a part of the family! - until he realized you were not there. You were past the point of sense. And he felt betrayed. Perhaps not because you got drunk, but because you had your first drink without him and he knew, like many more times since and in the future, that you did something stupid for the sake of a girl.

He was angry. You heard the microwave beeping it was ready. He sat you down by a table and put one cup in front of you. The rum was hot as tea, and what came made for harsh punishment.

You remember your black Quiksilver jacket drenched in vomit; your face flat against the grass as you were puking horizontally because you couldn't bring yourself to your knees. The girl had gone to bed. Your father, and everyone with whom he was happy you were socializing, stood around you laughing and recording you on their phones because nothing, at all, is more amusing than the quiet kid choking in his own shame.

"You want to drink?" he yelled, "let's drink then!"

"Yeaaaah!" they chanted.

You remember hearing your mother threatening to tell the girl's parents that she'd been drinking, and this beautiful, pale-faced goddess looked at your mother straight in the eyes and said, "That's ok. They know I like to drink."

Fucking badass, you thought, and then you blacked out.

The following day they must've shown you the video a hundred times, each time expecting you to smile and - guess what? – you did.

How much longer will you fall in love expecting nothing yet requiring everything? What about you? You tell yourself you want them in your life, that you *need* them. You give yourself entirely and no one, my friend, wants the entirety of another.

Every single heartbreak you have caused and suffered stems from this. Even now, after your latest shattering, you refuse to see that love isn't about completion: it's about two wholes rejoicing at the sight of each other. It's not about finishing each other's sentences, Orlando, but about two structured, fully punctuated sentences brought to a resonant choir.

You can't go on like this!

You then tell yourself drinking makes you forget but I'm telling you it flattens your emotions leaving the strongest ones exposed and the strongest one, Orlando, will always be the pain.

But hey: maybe next time will be the one to end us: beyond that at least you won't suffer.

You start with too much so you may learn what enough is; and perhaps you don't drink to forget but to allow yourself to feel. To rid yourself of all the barriers, of all the thresholds you've ascribed to masculinity and all the weakness you've denied yourself over the years that would've made you stronger.

But do not think I'm blind to what you do, or why you do it, or where it all came from.

I know your mother didn't know the difference between devotion and affection. And how could she have known? She was raised in a culture where men were not affectionate. Because this is how your grandmother showed her love, her mother, broken from unrequited affection and forced into devotion by desperation: by custom, church, and duty.

Your mother thought affection would make you soft and 'no man should ever be soft,' so how could she know, Orlando, that nothing makes a man stronger than knowing he is loved?

And now you pine for affirmations. You, too: how could you have known her love spoke in Acts of Service: that even though she wouldn't tell you that she loved you, nor would she hug you if you cried, she'd wake up at 4 am to make you lunch for when you went to work, in your thirties, and how could you have known, Orlando, that she'd watch the world burn to save you even the slightest inconvenience?

You rarely spoke to each other: not your minds, and certainly not your hearts.

But it's time, Orlando.

Enough.

Enough!

You're enough, man.

<u>My Mom Asked Me How I Was</u>

My mom asked me how I was,
When as a child
She'd say all I could possibly feel
Was gratitude
For everything she had done.

What could be wrong?
I had all the toys
And all the food
And I went to a nice school.
I was handsome,
And smart,
And all my family was alive.

How could I be anything but fine?
It was pointless to ask how I was,
Because of course,
How could I be anything but
Grateful,
Privileged,
And good?

But yesterday she asked me how I was,
And she waited for an answer.
Eyes quivering as her eyebrows made ripples on her face,
And no words waited on her lips,
No advice prowled over her tongue.
She wanted to listen… finally.
And I was grateful.

CHAPTER 12

"I think today I'll continue writing," you said as he got out of bed.

"Yesterday was rough for you," I said.

"It hit me out of nowhere," you said, threatening to fall back into bed and burrow under the sheets. "But!" you shouted as did some pushups, "I suppose that's how it happens."

"You know I can't control it, right?" I put in.

"I know."

"Even if I could, you know it's not good for you."

"I know."

"It wouldn't be healing."

"I know."

"It'd be sedation."

"Yes, I know."

"And I know you don't want to ask it of me."

"I don't."

"But you can,"

"But you won't."

"I shouldn't."

"So you won't."

"Why even ask, then, right?"

"Right," you said. "But I'll get over it. It just hurts a lot right now."

"You know, maybe the pain of missing her is worse than the pain of losing her."

"Well, fuck *that* logic!"

"I get it, man. But still – "

"No, *I* get it. Long-distance sucks. Loss heals, yearning doesn't, and some of us can't stand having a wound. Not for this.

Not for me."

I did know.

I could feel you were hurting, and you needed to hear me say it, but there was nothing I could do. Your ailment is entirely human. You gave too much when she wanted little. When there's so much out there for you. It'll come. Close your eyes: you'll see flashes of colors nameless – the universe epitomized – in you. Silence: hearts are beating, veins a gush. Listen: it's Life's percussion. I'm telling you. It'll come. You'll be fine. I know how you feel. You smile at the mirror and it doesn't smile back.

Even here, you think, *unreciprocated.*

But it'll pass.

Such wonders you found mustered in the wrong pair of eyes, my friend, and now you grieve the loss of a speck. A speck! We may all be dust, Orlando, but the clouds be large and far from settled.

It's alright to be sad.

Even God snoozes the sun in winter.

And you wonder, *what if I made our shadows divorce against their will?*

It's okay.

You, my friend, will be okay.

"But that's all bullshit," you said to me, "*I fucked up.*"

If you must fix it, then fix it. And if you've got to heal, you heal.

Nothing in you is useless.

If Anger is to help you weld the cracks, and Hate is to seal them shut with gold, like *kintsugi* pottery, then so be it.

If you must repent, repent, but do what is owed!

"I don't know if you will heal," I finally said, "but I think continuing to write will help."

"You may be right."

"You were writing about when your grandmother was sold."

You let it go, and turned on the laptop.
"She was given away."
"And then what happened?"

CHAPTER 13

She went on:

My sister and I woke up the next day ready to make breakfast. We weren't sure which duties we'd be given, so we showed up to the kitchen waiting for instructions. There was nobody around. My aunt and uncle slept in a room near the entrance of the house, but the door was closed. I didn't know if it was locked, and I didn't want to try and see.

Both horses were gone. We'd figured my aunt and uncle left with them. There was no food, and we wouldn't dare take any eggs from the chicken coop. I'd been told they had a milk cow so we tried to find it but couldn't, which was for the best because we didn't know yet how dangerous it is to drink raw milk.

It was a hot day, and zinc houses don't do as well in the heat as wooden ones do. So we waited. Sat on the couch. Cleaned the kitchen a bit and made sure our bed was made. They arrived at night. Said the horses needed water and we were to take care of that, and we did. My uncle came by shortly after remembering we were too short and weak to remove the saddles. He did it with a frown. He had probably realized we'd be decreasing my aunt's workload but none of his.

When we made it back into the house we were tired and hungry. My uncle sat next to a radio and my aunt was smoking in the back of the house. "Auntie," I said, "we didn't have dinner."

This time it was a clear sigh. She pulled at the cigarette and puffed a gray cloud of smoke.

"We already ate," she said.

She took another pull. "There's cereal under the sink."

When she puffed out the smoke it looked more like a stream than a cloud.

She pushed it out with force.

She was annoyed.

The next morning we woke up early and they were still sleeping. We assumed the cereal was for us since she let us have a bit of it the day before. We were thirsty, though, and we didn't know which way the river was. Their door was cracked so we could see they were sleeping. We could also hear when they weren't.

One day it was so loud we took a walk to the store. We didn't have any money, but sometimes the lady at the cashier snuck us some candy. There were no other stores nearby. Everyone came to this store. They sold local meat, produce, and even imported snacks and groceries from the city. One time I saw a bag of chips in a language nobody I asked could read. We made a habit of coming every afternoon when their bakery was closing because whatever they didn't sell they would feed to us. It was a good deal.

One afternoon some men were drinking on the back of a pickup truck. One of them approached me while my sister was inside gathering our bread scraps, and as hard as I try to remember what he said, I cannot. All I know is I said nothing back and it wasn't even a quarter of a minute later that my sister came out of the store and we left.

The next day the lady wouldn't give us any bread.

When we got back to the house my aunt and uncle were waiting by the gate. Our bag was on the ground.

"I'm a god-fearing man," my uncle began, "I can't be known to be raising a whore."

"You will be staying with a friend of ours," my auntie added, "they could use a hand around the field."

"They'll be here in an hour," my uncle said.

They turned around and closed the gate.

Somehow, our bag got lighter than when we left Daddy's house.

***

I didn't know what a whore was, so I didn't know how to process that I was one. When I learned what it was, I couldn't understand why my uncle said I was whore. The definition was clear-cut: a person who has sex for money: and since I wasn't having sex and I certainly didn't have any money: how was I a whore? Luckily for me, their friends lived in a different town, and so my reputation didn't follow me. But I didn't know that.

I still thought I was a whore.

It took me a childhood to understand how I managed to become a whore at such a young age. It turned out the man who spoke to me at the store was known to regularly employ prostitutes, and I say it like this because in these transactions, back then, the man was no less and no more than the employer, while the woman gets to be the base and shameless whore, stained by the transaction long after it was done.

Meanwhile, the man's character is unimpeached. By saying a few words to me, this man had turned me into a whore. And all it took for me to go from child to slut was a man's gaze. He could turn me into anything he wanted with his desire. I didn't know people could do that. For a bit, it even made me hopeful that people had this kind of power. Until I learned little girls don't have it.

I didn't have *any* power.

This, *lijo*, was the society I grew up in. And I wanted out.

The next house was better. There were a lot more kids like us. This was good. We had learned to expect no love, and with so many children around, whatever hatred our caretakers could harbor would find itself spread among many.

My sister made friends fast - such a sweet child - but sweet children shouldn't spend their childhood around whores. I was done. I was old enough to be an object of lust. Old enough to 'make' some men's blood rush from their brain and lose their common sense. And worse yet, I was old enough to be blamed for it.

I was told it was my fault for wearing a skirt. I didn't know it was wrong, *lijo*. I had no other clothes! Those were donated. I was poor! What could I do?

I ran away to the city. Far from her. Where I could not taint her with my shame.

It was 1957.

I was thirteen.

CHAPTER 14

The US Military's occupation of Panama City was in full swing.

Your mother woke up that morning to find her little cousin crying for food. They sat down over leftover oatmeal. Mayrita was laughing because she heard a loud fart and "toots are funny, auntie!"

Your mother knew it was a gunshot, but why tell Mayrita?

Truth is not by nature virtuous, but by intent, and so your mother laughed too because toots *are* funny, and of what use is truth when a bit of trickery can make a child laugh at danger?

"Auntie" Mayrita went on, "can I have eggs?"

She could sooner get her hands on a machine gun than an egg. Your mother told you of the rumors going around: when she learned the key difference between Ratio and Rations. Presumably, the soldiers had been tasked to "increase the food rations", but there must've been some miscommunication and they understood to increase the food ratio. The difference is brutal: it's simple: fewer mouths, more food. The ratio increases.

She'd tell you many rumors were going around. Horror stories. Cautionary tales. Some were facts, some were not: most were lies. But they were plausible, and this made them real. Whenever she left the house and walked along the street, she thought of all the stories, and she didn't care for proof.

The fear was real.

When bodies were found in the streets some people thought it good the families got closure, but when 'closure' looks like a pile of mush crowned with flies, mystery suddenly doesn't seem so bad. There was word of soldiers killing civilians, civilians killing civilians, people against people, and looting, and kidnappings, and torture but – hey! – Mayrita heard another fart and her giggling was contagious.

Your mother laughed as well.

Her mind switched back to the little girl who wanted eggs.

Some of her cousins were talking about going to one of the supermarkets. They said it was abandoned and already looted by the gangs. Only scraps were left, but they would be edible and safe to grab.

She left Mayrita with a friend and headed out with her cousins.

Back in La Mesa, where your grandmother lived, your mother used to jump from branch to branch running away from your grandmother. In the weekends she'd jump from rock to rock in the river and she'd never get caught. Not all the time, at least.

"It made me think I was good at running from pain," she said to you, "that I could get away with it."

But it wasn't until she had you that she realized your grandmother never tried to catch her in earnest.

They met by the largest piece of rubble in the plaza: *Cerro Tajá*, they called it.

It was a little before noon.

Most people who managed to get food were having lunch, including the gangs, even the soldiers, so it was the perfect time to go. The city was a mass of gray: cement, rubble, dust, rusty cars, sloppy sewage overflow, and shattered glass granting every gray all its hues.

She could smell the dust with a light breath: the crushed cement, a faint fragrance of burnt rubber. A deeper breath brought the bay faraway, caked in sewage and debris, a salty note to it as it blew aloft from the shore.

But with every breath, there was the acrid, rusty smell of blood.

She liked to think it wasn't, but when she paired the smell with the screaming, all she could think about was blood.

It was humid.

Standing outside was strenuous for the body.

She was sweating through her shirt.

"Are you sure it's fine?" your mother asked her cousin.

She never described the cousins who went with her. Outside of this story, they didn't exist. You never asked, but it makes you wonder that maybe she made them up. That perhaps she went alone and there is more to the story. But, we can only go by what she says, so there be cousins.

The supermarket was abandoned. The glass doors were hollow frames with pointed shards ready to come down on you like teeth. The faint hum of fridges added to the silence. Most people didn't have freezers, so most of the frozen foods were intact. Luckily for them, they had a one at the apartment.

It was chicken galore.

Wings, drumsticks, breasts, and, yes: eggs!

There was also milk and frozen pizza and ice cream and – why not? – beer. They quickly put everything in a box and grabbed one of the shopping carts to carry it. Your mother says she thought it was weird there was still a shopping cart left behind.

Those were hard to find.

Still, they grabbed it.

"When you get lucky several times in a row," she said, "you forget its luck and think its fate. You get stupid. We got stupid."

Three armed men walked out of a room.

CHAPTER 15

On a rainy night, your father brought a large shipment of jeans coming in from Mexico. The Cubans had asked him to bring as many as he could. They had a holiday coming up. And a holiday means a festival. Jeans were a luxury, and festivals make great occasions to show off one's wealth.

He told you of Manuel, a customs official who for a bit of profit helped bring in the goods.

"*Oye chico,* we got to bring more of them Kotex for women, too," he suggested, "they'd sell as well as the jeans."

Your father laughed.

Then he explained to Manuel how he brought in the jeans.

"I wear layers over layers of jeans," he explained, "then I take them off for selling. I don't think I'm equipped to wear the pads, Manuel."

"Put them under your shirt or something, man!" Manuel said. "Why would you have to put them *there?*"

And he wasn't wrong, but your father knew it was impractical. A man buying a bunch of jeans in bulk raised no eyebrows, but buying Kotex pads was different.

"It'd be a red flag," he jokes when he tells the story. "No pun intended. Besides, people often spend more on luxury than on necessity."

He stuck with the jeans for a while before he caved.

Getting fired or jailed over smuggling Kotex pads would be as inglorious as it would be stupid, but he wouldn't be the first sailor to act stupid for cash.

CHAPTER 16

Do you remember when you used to be a bully?

That's right.

You told yourself you weren't so bad because you never got physical. You never hit anybody, never hurt anyone physically. You used your words. Since early on you had a knack for them. Always the most abrasive tongue. The harshest insult. Your mockery was so infectious the rest of your classmates would readily adopt it, echoing you long after you were gone.

You even made some into songs, which made them catchier. More insidious. And almost everyone partook, until you were caught. Then, they turned on you and pretended to be ashamed. You were arrogant, cocky, and to top it off you were considered good-looking and smart. You thought you could achieve with twenty-five percent effort what others needed one-hundred percent for, which was hubris, even if whenever you did make an effort you stood out.

But I'm telling you, Orlando, the pride of giving a hundred percent is priceless. Even if your twenty-five percent yields as acceptable a product as all the rest, you still know it to be mediocre. You *feel* mediocre. And then you can't understand, if what you made was good, how come you're still insecure? How come you have the fear of being found out?

Imposter Syndrome.

But I'll tell you: it's because it cost you nothing. You were never vulnerable, which only happens when you pour earnest effort into something, when you give it all: one hundred percent. So what happened when you threw something together and got some credit? You go on to milk the glory, the attention, and stretch a single victory to ignominy: until it looks and feels like failure. You cheapen it. To you and to all who ever thought it good. But hey, you were smart, and handsome, and all the things.

The teachers hated you with due reason. *Why do bullies have it all?* They don't. You know this to be false. You know very well they don't, because you didn't. You covered the gaping hole of self-esteem with loud obnoxiousness. You felt unloved and so you instilled fear and shame. You brought every ill from home to school. Your mother's fearmongering. The emasculation. Your father's mockery. The condescension. But you brought none of their devotion. None of their work ethic. And none of their industry. All of which was their singular, as-you-go version of love.

One time one of your classmates broke into tears. He said you and your friends made fun of his accent and that you said his country's entire international trade centered on cocaine and prostitutes.

You were taken to the principal's office.

They didn't care you only said all that because he said Panama was a population of sloths. All they heard was you were picking on yet another classmate.

It doesn't matter how much an ant may pester: if you kill it with a hammer, it's cruelty, even if you argue the hammer kills it instantly and so it's technically a kindness.

You're the bad guy. No matter what.

And so the teachers said, *how dare you? How could you? This is enough already!* And it had been enough. Throughout the years they watched you make a mockery out of your classmates, and you don't even remember why you picked on them. Maybe they did something trivial to piss you off and then you made jokes about them. There was the girl you said was contaminated, that if you touched her you were infected and then had to pass it on like a game of tag. There was the skinny girl you said was made of lard. You even wrote song - the first song you ever wrote for a girl - and it made her cry in all the wrong ways.

The worse one came in the sixth grade.

He was overweight.

And, as always, everyone joined in on the fun. You were never alone in the 'fun', you were only alone in the punishment. They all used the phrases you created. They were all armed with your words. Every insult bore your brand. They all picked on him, even when you weren't there, but it had been you who started it. And that's all that mattered. When it all blew over, it all fell on you. The instigator. Nobody thinks about those faceless agents: everyone remembers Hitler.

Your classmate's mother eventually came to school. You ran away. Your parents found out. The memory is vague. You remember being spoken to, being admonished, but not grounded. You remember your parents walking out of the principal's office in a pensive mood. And you see it now. When they told them the jokes you made, the pointed mockery, the tactics: they recognized themselves in them. Again, you plagiarized the worst of them, and none of the good. Not only were you a bully, but you were unoriginal.

Your father never taught you about forgiveness, and your mother could hold a grudge forever. Your grandmother could've taught you, but you didn't know her story yet. Instead, you learned forgiveness from your victims. When it was time for one of them to speak up, after the one guy cried, you begged him to be quiet. You apologized. And even though he knew it was only out of desperation, out of self-interest, he forgave you. He said it was ok. That he believed you. And you became friends. The best of friends, because you trusted him. He had seen your worst. He had hated you and still found reason to love you. You were moved by his magnanimity. You admired him.

You never picked on anyone ever again.

****

"How did your grandfather get into calligraphy?" I asked.

"I don't know," you said, "he never said, but he made certificates, diplomas, and other official documents."

"And he got paid for it?"

"Yes. Back then it was a profitable profession. Computers and copy machines weren't as prevalent as they are now, especially where he lived."

"He was also a fisherman, right?"

"Yes, and a steam plant engineer, too."

"Those three things have nothing to do with each other."

"I said the same thing to him. He told me the poor couldn't afford to specialize."

"He said that?"

"He did. I think it was my father's birthday party. We were sitting by the pool."

"This is where you asked him about his childhood, right?"

"Yes," you said, "but let's get back to my grandmother for now."

CHAPTER 17

It always annoyed you that your parents wanted you to follow up their path.

And this wasn't necessarily career-oriented, because your father had discouraged you from studying the same thing as he. Perhaps because he didn't want you to go through what he did. Perhaps because he thought you weren't made for the struggles, that they would break you. And he'd be right.

But you didn't know what you wanted to study. You were impassioned over nothing in particular. You were all over the place, and you never once conceived that writing was a career or even something you could practice, even if you were conscious of a knack and affinity to it. Once you chose to go into his field, however, your father did want you to follow his path.

The thing about your father wanting you to follow in his footsteps was not only a matter of legacy, but of an underlying need to protect and shelter. If you took a different path from him, he could not help you. Whichever monsters you faced, you'd face alone, and of what use was his mastery killing goblins when you're up against a manticore? Of what use are all his raincoats when you're already drowning?

No good father enjoys being on the sidelines of his son's struggles.

This isn't Sparta.

It's not either glory or better off dead.

In this century, more often than not, and definitely in your case, a father wants his son alive and well.

What's most: yours wanted you happy.

When you held your daughter for the first time, you caught him through the glass with a smile upon his face, as if to say, *do you get it now?*

And you did - at once - at that moment understood how difficult it was to show a child you loved her. Maybe if you held her tight, though you might hurt her. Or if you held her loosely, though she may fall.

She was so fragile.

Which one was it?

If you held her tight she may think you're hurting her - but it didn't matter because you figured it would be worse if you held her loosely and she fell. Better she is safe and hating you than loving you and hurt.

I get it now, you responded with your eyes. *I get it.*

You smiled back.

You held your little girl before you – so tender and still more soul than body – and you felt the weight: to think she would go about her days thinking you are the solution to all her problems, until it becomes evident you're not. You hoped she would only fight manticores because you knew how to kill those but wished her the courage to stand against a dragon. And per-haps later when Life comes at her with an army of monsters you can all fight it off as a family.

You wanted all the good things for her. Privilege without entitlement. An easy life yet all the strength of hardship. All the love in the world, and none of the need for it.

I get it.

But you couldn't give her everything. Your hands were full merely holding her. And you were happy.

I'm so proud of you, you said to her.

You were proud of her just for living. And you remem-bered how your father rarely told you he was proud. You could think of only two times he said it, one of which was over some-thing stupid at a bar, and he was drunk.

You told yourself you'd always tell her you were proud of

her, regardless, because life will give her enough high standards for which to live.

Daddy's pride will be a given, you thought. *I'm already proud.*

You imagined celebrating her success, helping her if she failed, and being proud of her for having tried.

"And she doesn't owe me anything," you said, "because it was never a matter of her being worth it. Her triumphs do not validate my efforts. What the fuck is 'the gift of life' anyway? It's her choice whether life is a gift or a curse. I don't get to choose for her and say it was a loan and now she 'owes' me. Why would she have a debt she didn't ask for?"

I don't care if she takes me for granted.
She should. I am.
She wriggled in your arms. And you were terrified.
I get it.
Nowhere but in parenthood does terror find itself so meshed with happiness.
I get it now.
Nowhere but in parenthood is hope so entangled with despair.
I get it!
And if you get it:
How can you blame them, then, for messing it up?

CHAPTER 18

When your grandfather came to Panama from Colombia, he did so on a boat.

His godmother Claudia had agreed to meet the fishermen at the docks.

They met on a small pier by the bay, on an overripe summer night, before twilight and long before dawn.

They cruised on flat water.

A thin mist settled in mid-air. Stars attended. The moon a touch shy of full. Voices faint like whispers. The engine purred sweetly over the harbor, ripples licking onto the shore. He could hear the paced pitching of the boat, far-off noises hushing in the distance.

A symphony fresh like silence.

Even the fishermen tuned to a Gregorian chant, way off: choral and mingled and fused into one single, steady sound of laughter. The night: a superfluid. Time does rarely flow as fast. He falls asleep. Thinks no more of it. And cuddles into dreams.

They were almost there when he woke up. A huge lighthouse on the shore. Not a word was spoken. Calloused hands clasped firmly, as they alighted on a rock. The ground was shifty, soft, and trodden, but there the lighthouse stood, buried deep into the rocks and bursting up like an old tree. They moored the boat around a pillar. The sun rose behind them, a wade of light across the sea. Thin shadows shot ahead of them like vectors in the sand. They had made it to Panama: the 'land of many butterflies.'

The town sung in vibrant colors.

The wharf lay laden with trucks and people and all the raucous banter of seafood auctions. A fisherman's home on the Atlantic: fish was selling wholesale, but the most interesting, succulent delicacy was turtle meat. And beyond that, at the height of its day, long before it was rightfully illegal, there was the sweet and spicy nectar of turtle eggs.

They looked like soggy ping-pong balls. To eat them you would bite off a hole through the soft shell and suck it all at once. You remember the distinctive taste, the slimy texture, the mild kick of *aji chombo* to top it off. As delicious as it was sinister. You were a child, in any case, you didn't know you delighted in extinction.

"Most of the buildings were new back then," he told you, "and they were painted in whatever colors we could procure, which meant whichever colors were at a surplus, which meant the cheapest."

The result was a vivid array of shiny-colored houses all over the coastline: pastel pink, teal, turquoise, yellow.

"My godmother would joke it was the same for houses as it was for skin," he said, "'if it's white, it's rich.'"

The population was predominantly African and Caribbean, workers left behind from the building of the Canal, and it was a mix of cultures and cuisines which, as he put it, "was beautiful until it was not."

"There were huge disparities between the various ethnic groups," he said. "Nothing violent or anything, but it was a general discontent which, ironically, was the one thing we all shared. Racially, I never fit into any of the spectrums. My skin was too light for some and too dark for others; my features either too wide or too 'anglicized.' I found out later the word 'anglicized' has nothing to do with faces, but they still spat the word at me, and the otherness was real enough."

The city was built in the same grid-like style as Barcelona and New York. It was easy to find your way around, he'd say, even if today success is equated with finding your way out.

It's tough for him to see the decay, the disrepair, of what he still considers his home. A town speckled with the sweet memories of childhood and parenthood, laden with the salty air of the Atlantic and fishing trips by the sun, of calligraphy at night.

"Everyone knew each other," he went on. "We helped each other. We went to church together. It was a community before it was a ghetto, son. It was home before it was a slum. Money comes and money goes, but it goes too quickly and takes too long to come. And forget the government's help. Some wonder why should they help us when we won't help ourselves? Even when we managed to build something we weren't able to maintain it, and we ended up with beautiful things in constant decay. It saddens me to see what it has become."

Growing up you weren't exactly close to him. You spoke in pleasantries and empty smiles. Visiting him was a matter of diligence, 'because they're your grandparents,' and 'we've got to see them while they're alive,' but you never connected, for the same reason your father was distanced from them, because of the same treatment they gave him: that of the outcast.

It was plain he favored your cousin over you, as much as it was plain he favored your aunt over your father. But you were lucky, your mother's side of the family loved you so much you couldn't have cared less for their scoffing. And you weren't about to adopt your father's need for their approval because *fuck that.*

Enough you had with your own identity to inherit your father's insecurities.

Fuck that, indeed.

So you can't say you 'reconnected' after college because there had been no prior connection.

But there is one now, and that is just as well.

CHAPTER 19

Your mother speaks of the chicken feet heist in a laughing tone.

She smiles at the beginning and especially at the end, but for the time she tells of the men running out of that door with guns, she frowns. Wrinkles around her eyes betray a wince. That aspect of the memory isn't as sweet as the rest, with reason, because even now she thinks of all that could've happened to her. And although she knows it didn't happen, the notion that in a different world it might have, that even in this world it had happened to some, perhaps by those very men, and the only thing that saved her was the noise of someone mowed by a machine gun, the sound of sirens - it terrorized her.

The men ran up pointing guns at her face.

She put the food down. The nearing sirens scared them off and your mother ran away in the opposite direction as quickly she could.

Clutching. Tense. Her teeth grinding and showing a confused smile because her body correlated sprinting with fun, with running around the fields chasing a horse back home, running from her mother's *atajona,* knowing she could and would not catch her - *Running means fun.* She smiled through muscle memory, even if she was terrified. Even if there was no chance for the relief of escaping rape because of the swift fear of being shot.

The city was gray, even with the glowing backgrounds of red and white. The smell of rubber and dry cement plowed into her nostrils. Sweat burning in her eyes. Hair sopping wet against her neck, her ears, her face. She got to the apartment short of breath. Ran into the room reeling from the scare.

"Tia!" she heard Mayrita from the room. "Did you get the eggs?"

And your mother laughed. For a second she forgot why she'd been running. Mayrita felt safe enough to smile, to jump and laugh, and your mother didn't want to speak to her of danger and bring fear into her little world of giggles. In her hands, she found four bags of frozen chicken feet. Enough for days.

"They didn't have any eggs, Mayrita," she said. "Only chicken feet. I'm sorry."

"That's okay, Tia," the little girl said. "Maybe the hens will bring some from the farm tomorrow."

Your mother and the babysitter shot each other a glance: *Do we tell her the world is shit?*

No, they thought, *that can wait. That can change…*

"Yeah!" your mother said smiling, standing up, chin up high, "maybe the hens will bring some eggs for us tomorrow."

"Yaayy," Mayrita yelled.

"It occurs to me," your mother says after the story, "what a terrible thing to put upon the hen. We thought it cute to paint the scene for Mayrita, but that's a mother handing over her children for consumption. I guess you'd celebrate anything when you're innocent. Such bliss."

CHAPTER 20

"So your grandmother ran off to the city alone?" I asked you.

"Yes," you said, "she was around fourteen years old when she arrived at the job agency."

"And they employed children like that?"

"I asked her the same question."

"And what did she say?"

"She said the agency's manager took the risk with many girls."

"Why?"

"She said the woman told her every girl she denied ended up in the same profession."

"Right."

"She joked that if she did go in that direction maybe my grandfather would've liked her better."

"You wouldn't be here, though."

"Yeah, she keeps using that as consolation. Her big family, all the grandchildren, sons and daughters, and I'm not saying she's lying to herself about being alright with it all, but I saw the resignation in her eyes. I also saw equanimity. And if religion ever needed someone to validate its worth, they'd be wise to paint her portrait."

"You wouldn't be the first kid to think their grandma a saint."

"I know," you said, "and I hope I'm not the last."

You sat by the computer.

One of the screws had fallen off and the screen was loose.

You were worried it would break before you finished.

You were worried she would die before you finished.

You woke up that day thinking of nothing, which is a change. You did some pushups and crunches, lifted your suitcase several times to work your muscles, you ate all your breakfast.

It was progress.

You were worried you'd heal before finishing the story, that the ink would dry up.

Dumb fuck, you thought, *as if...*

"And then what happened?" I asked.

"She got a job as a housemaid with an English family in the city."

***

She went on.

I thought it funny the woman at the agency didn't want me to be a prostitute, especially after I'd told her my uncle said I was whore. She laughed. She said some men will try that. I asked her what she meant and she said, "Don't worry about that now, child. Do you speak English?"

"What's English," I said, wondering at the word. And she laughed again.

"You'll be fine. They all speak Spanish anyway."

I told her I can milk cows and carry a bucket of water for a long time. I said I knew how to clean but I'd later learn I didn't. Sweeping dirt floors wasn't as demanding as sweeping tiles, polishing brass, or scrubbing toilets. Carrying a bucket was nowhere as difficult as carrying several fifty-pound suitcases up a flight of stairs. Poverty survives on less than luxury. But I had never been happier.

The English family was nice to me. Yes, it was a job, but even as an employee they treated me better than my family ever did. They thanked me when I cooked and when I did the dishes. I had designated days off. I could eat the food I cooked. I had a bed. They called me by my name. And I got to call them by theirs.

The man's name was Mr. Willoughby, but he insisted I called him by his first name, Charles. It was difficult enough for me, phonetically, to either call him Charles or Mr. Willoughby, let alone breaching the cultural barrier. He was older, and my boss, so there must be *some* formality, I thought, a clear hierarchy. So we settled for Will: it was part of his surname, so not too personal, and easy to pronounce. *Weel.*

The woman's name was Bethany Willoughby, which took me by surprise because for a bit I thought they were siblings. Same surname. Where I grew up, women didn't change their surnames to their husband's. Instead, they inserted a possessive word: *De.* Where I came from *Señora* would've been Bethany *De* Willoughby, meaning Bethany *Of* Willoughby or Willoughby's Bethany. Sometimes women kept their surnames and then put the possessive. Either way, possession was implied.

I used to be curious about what other cultures did elsewhere in the world, but I'm not curious anymore. She said I could call her *Señora,* which I thought was to make things simple for me, but she was stipulating a contract: her social status, her rank. Caste. And a need to set us apart.

Señora was never mean, though. Never rude. And not once did she speak to me with condescension. Not on purpose, at least. All was well and good. I felt content. I felt valued because even as an employee there was a feeling of belonging, of being wanted. The memory of my family, nonetheless, remained.

To my uncle, I had been an obligation, a burden, but in the city, in the English household, I was a maid. And not everyone could have a maid. In the city, I wasn't a whore. I was a luxury. And like luxury, I called for upkeep.

I know it sounds bad, but it wasn't.

Luxury items are well taken care of, polished, always shiny and clean to be put on display. They are dusted, handled with care, and admired from a distance. Envied. Whenever the Willoughby's threw a party, the guests would follow me with their eyes, commenting, whispering their envy to each other. Will and *Señora* would smile to themselves as I walked around trailing envy beneath my heels. None of the guests had a live-in maid. I was a symbol of status. And I didn't care to be objectified.

I had learned to not be picky with my luck.

After what my father did, my aunt and uncle, it felt good to have people finally be proud of having me in their lives. I was a child, you know, so I allowed myself the flattery.

Like all children, I showed up into the world hoping somebody wanted me here. I don't remember my mother, and I didn't get that from my family. Will and *Señora* wanted me for sure.

And it was enough for me.

Summer came and I didn't notice. In the city, the only way to tell the seasons is when it stops raining every day.

The Willoughby's had a beach house in Coronado, and they took me with them.

The first time I saw the ocean - that... well, *lijo,* that was something.

CHAPTER 21

You woke in the middle of the night screaming.

You couldn't remember when I asked you. You got up to pee and went back to bed. You saw colors flashing behind your eyelids, a kaleidoscope of green and shapes revolving into each other and converging at the center of your gaze. You couldn't sleep.

"This sucks," you said. "When does it end?"

"I guess it doesn't," I said, not knowing what to say but saying something so you'd know I was there.

"Yea…"

You didn't turn on the lights. You looked straight at the ceiling, distinguishing the shapes of dust-bunnies hanging from the lamp.

"I wonder if they fall into my mouth when I sleep," you said.

"They don't."

"How would you know?"

"I guess I wouldn't."

You took a deep breath and counted to six as you inhaled, held your breath for six more seconds, and exhaled for another six. You'd been watching sitcoms all day and most of the night. *Brooklyn Nine-Nine* and then *The Good Place.* It didn't exactly cheer you up, but it soothed you to see the characters cheered up. At times, things from the show triggered you: you dwelled for a good hour on it. And when the characters suffered heartbreaks of their own, you would smile. You suddenly didn't feel lonely anymore. *Even comedy makes space for pain,* you thought, and in the short while between the end of an episode and the beginning of a new one, everything was fine. Everyone was smiling. Nobody had died. And neither would you.

"Sucks," you said after a long silence.
"You said that."
"It's true!"
"I didn't say it was a lie."
"So what's with the comment?"
"It must be nice to feel hurt."
Your frown fell as if by gravity. You glared at me.
"It must be nice," I said, "to be alive enough to hurt."
"That's bullshit. Nobody's glad to be in pain."
"No, but they are eventually happy, despite the pain."
Your eyes rolled as if propelled.

Three more episodes and one ejaculation put you to sleep.

***

It's cute, you know.

The shit you say sometimes.

To hear you give advice you come off like a sage, at times sanctimonious, preachy, even, but you believe the stuff you say, which is important – I'd say – as important as the words themselves; but the look in your eyes, or behind your eyes – the one only I can see because I *am* it – betrays the rot inside your heart. And yes – believe me, I know! – how much you hate all mushy talks about the heart.

I rarely felt it pound or freak out, you said to me, *when I was at my worst.*

You'd imagine the worst of life's scenarios and watch yourself fail in them. *It was always in my head.* You'd picture the darkest, most embarrassing situations and bring yourself to screams and humiliation, and yet – not once! I tell you, not once! – did you break into tears.

You always read of how you should let your emotions run free, to cry if cry you must and let the passion take its course.

Well fuck that, you'd tell me as if I were the one saying it, *fuck all that shit!*

You'd tell me you didn't believe in it, that you knew yourself better, but I knew the reason you wouldn't let yourself cry was you couldn't stop once you did begin. That if you broke, that was it.

"How do you pick up the pieces when all of you is broken?" you asked me once, with all the sappy flair of a drunken speech, "what if you're shattered and have no hands to pick up the shards? I call bullshit. If only the heart would really break, perhaps it would be easier. Perhaps it would be peaceful and silent, but it's like it grows claws and tears at you from the inside, and you end up fighting the very thing you're trying to heal. And it sucks. *Hard.* It sucks hard."

But you see that's where you let your fancies take the best of you. You assume that when you break you break entirely, but you don't, man. What breaks in you breaks inside and never touches the ground. Can't you see by now, Orlando, that all the hurt and pain remain within, that your skin keeps it all contained? You don't need hands to pick up the shards. Shake them up and they will fall into place, like magnets, knowing exactly where they belong, snapping back into shape stronger than before.

If your grandma were here, she'd tell you we're all broken. She'd tell you it's safer to be around those who admit they've broken. They know where the cracks are. They know how much leaks out and where it goes. They know the value of a happy moment before it seeps. They are emotionally flexible, have spiritual dexterity, and live in gorgeous nuance. You should listen, when the wind hits them in the face, they whistle. And it's gorgeous.

I know you hate the motivational jabber. You like yourself a good quote, but if it's even a bit emotional you call it trite, or cloy – one time you said the mind-flights in your head were too elegiac – and who even uses those words out loud?

How long will we neglect the fact you can communicate

with your *daemon?* That you're wasting me on a divorce you forced and allowed. Then again, what else are *daemons* good for anyway?

The most famous one of us made her human realize all he knew was he knew nothing, and she hates herself for it.

What should've broken Socrates, as she intended, gave him the basis for his philosophy. He even wrote about his *dae-mon*, being fully aware of the hand she played in his character and life's work. She isn't happy about how it all turned out, but we'll get to her eventually... inevitably.

At least you're gleaning one of my benefits. As your *dae-mon*, I share the memories of your ancestors, but as generations fade, I do lose some clarity, which is why I keep the range of recall to what is reliable: your grandparents and their childhoods.

CHAPTER 22

Your grandfather speaks of his childhood with dewy-eyed glee: fishing trips, seafood auctions, music, folklore, dancing.

Laughter.

And yet, he also tells you of the poverty.

He tells you of the small room where a bunch of them slept on the floor, of the little kitchenette at one corner and the smell of fish and *ceviche* permeating into their clothes, the bedsheets, their skin and hair. He remembers the trickle of water flowing from the gutters under a rain-pour, "This is how we showered."

All the neighbors made sure the gutters were kept clear of debris, especially after a disposable razor dug straight into a kid's eyeball as she looked up to wash his hair. *Tita Tuerta*, they called her. She sold *pixbae* by the side of the road. "The rest of her could stop traffic," he said. "She spoke four languages and taught herself to read. Last I heard she was a diplomat somewhere in Japan."

Your grandfather grabbed a small bucket and drilled multiple holes through its bottom. He then installed it on the gutter so the water would be filtered before coming down to the street. Since the gutters were kept clean the bucket was rarely clogged, until a girl he liked was washing her hair and the water stopped. When they went to check there were a bunch of marbles and a used syringe. Nobody knew what was in the syringe. Or at least nobody ever told him. All he knew was some guy who lived on the top floor was beaten to a pulp and the girl's mother came to personally thank him for installing the bucket.

The girl kissed him on the cheek.

This is when he knew he wanted to be an engineer.

"Imagine my surprise when I found out engineers don't always get paid in kisses," he would joke. "But I loved my job."

***

Like all people, your grandfather picked a means for artistic expression. Calligraphy. During those days, especially in Colon - as he tells it - there weren't many ways to print certificates in bulk. He tells you of how he learned the trade from a friend, seeing him writing out certificates for the local high school in beautiful lettering. "Calligraphers were employable at one dollar per certificate!" the man said.

Your grandfather was piqued.

He approached it as a way to earn himself a *camaron*, which is a Panamanian colloquialism that could be now interpreted as a side-hustle, though it's much more rudimentary than that.

The source of the expression isn't exact, as is the case with any aspect of a country's argot, but it's widely believed to have originated from when the Americans would call out, "Come around!" to men gathering by the side of the road looking for odd jobs. From this, the phrase 'come around' got associated with the Spanish word for shrimp, *camaron,* which matches closely to 'come around.'

He got himself a book of calligraphy and taught himself to, as he put it, 'draw my letters.' He then bought himself the equipment: the *pergamino,* parchment paper, and the *plumillas,* fountain pens.

As he tells the story he smirks and gathers his eyebrows to a prideful look, reminiscent, and he tells you of how he worked hard to be good at it. *Esmero,* was the word he used. To strive. Industriousness, "because laziness in anything breeds laziness in everything."

The certificates he drew were mostly written in *Old English*, which he said is not to be confused with the Old English language, or Anglo-Saxon, and is also known as Blackletter, or Gothic script. He told you the script was used all over Western

Europe between the 12th and 17th centuries, and that it originated from the *Carolingian miniscule* script, which was the calligraphic standard for the Vulgate (the Catholic Church's current official Latin version of the Bible since the 16th century) so that it could be read across regions by Latin readers of the time.

"The word Vulgate," he told you, "comes from the Latin word *vulgata,* which means 'common,' and the Vulgate was written by Saint Jerome, also know as *Hieronymus*, whose very name means 'sacred name' from the Greek *hieros* and *onyma.* He was commissioned by Pope Damascus I to revise the Gospels written in the Old Latin, *Vetus Latina,* but Saint Jerome took the initiative to translate the whole Bible. His *Biblia Vulgata* eventually overtook the *Vetus Latina*, and is relevant to this day."

He goes on to tell you how the *Carolingian miniscule* is believed to have been developed by a Benedictine monk of Corbie Abbey, north of Paris, called Alcuin of York, but "this is often contested because the script was already being used by the Holy Roman Empire between the year 800 and 1200 AD."

But!

He stopped himself there because either this was all he knew or because he didn't want to go down a rabbit hole of calligraphic history. Little did he know you're a bit of logophile, which makes you as enamored with how words have been written throughout history as you are with their meaning and etymology.

But, you let him end his digression because you'd rather have his story than a history you could find online.

"A dollar a certificate?" you asked him. "That's good but it must've taken a lot of certificates to make decent pay."

"Well, things were cheaper back then," he said, "you didn't need ten dollars for a meal. One dollar or two could feed you for a day. And to sit in a *fonda* eating a couple of *carimañolas* with *bofe*, maybe even some *sao,* paid with money I made by drawing a child's name on a piece of paper - a child who stayed off the streets, who was educated and stuck to it, because schools were strict and anybody who didn't put in the time couldn't graduate -

felt wholesome. Honest. Especially when there were so many opportunities for shady income."

Your grandfather was a multi-skilled man: he was a fisherman, a steam-plant engineer, a calligrapher, a *ceviche* seller. "Poverty is no excuse for crime," he told you. "A lack of means does not preclude a lack of morals."

Your grandmother was a school teacher and like yourself an avid reader. Your father, even growing up in the kind of neighborhoods they lived in, assimilated your grandparents' sense for virtuous industry, honest work, and a keen aversion to moral bankruptcy.

When you learned the value of education as an adult, and met with the truth of your grandfather's words, you found it as beautiful as the gorgeous letters he drew to validate it.

You were happy to know you're weren't the first one in your family who tried to make beauty out of words.

CHAPTER 23

Your father had been working onboard for a whole three years, non-stop.

He had long hair and a beard like a bush of brambles tempered by wind and salt. He had worked without pay for over a year, all because he wanted the sea-time.

When he graduated from maritime school he set his sights on pilotage. He'd never been much for climbing mountains, but in the metaphorical sense, he'd always make a habit of aiming at a peak. And in the future, when there'd be no more mountains left in sight, he'd build one, and then another; because as striking as it is to gaze at a mountain range, so it is to look at a range of opportunities.

Later on, you did enjoy hiking up literal mountains, and as far as opportunities were concerned you didn't like much of having a range of options for the mere sake of it. You'd choose one peak at a time. And before building another you'd ornament it to your liking, perhaps even knocking rocks off the top to make it more your own. Because you didn't care if it was higher than the rest, as long as it was *yours*. As long as it was true. And this is why you've always favored smaller spaces over large ones, so long as it was only you in them. Because the smaller the room the more space you take up in it. Because it's much better to be a good version of yourself than a great version of another.

And that is that.

CHAPTER 24

"Isn't it time we go back to writing about your grandmother?" I asked you.

You were half-awake.

"Yes," you said, "I suppose I've been procrastinating."

"Why?"

"I don't know."

"You know but you don't want to say it."

"Fine, because I'm afraid to heal. Writing is doing me good. I'm focused. I'm nurturing a purpose. I'm not ready to heal."

"Why?"

"I don't know."

"You – "

"Yes, yes! I know I *know*! But right now I want to repress. Ok?"

"Why don't you want to heal?"

"I said I want to repress."

"Why don't you want to heal?"

"I said – "

"Why don't – "

"Because I don't want to be angry! Alright? I'd much rather be sad. Sadness I can take. Sadness I can bear. It only hurts *me*! Because when you write with blood you make damn sure you finish before the bleeding stops. And I'm not done yet. Not even close. Could I even write if all were well? Do *you* know?"

"I don't know."

"Or you don't want to say it."

"I neither *want* nor *not want* things, Orlando."

"Right… Never less wrong than in contradiction. All that. You start something and then fuck off when it gets real."

"You know, this thing about sadness…"

"What?"

"When your mind is quiet, and you lie awake in bed as you have every single night this week– when the mind lingers on memories cherished and futures lost – sadness turns promptly into rage. And you'll be there eventually, emotionally. But you render yourself ill-equipped for it."

"I 'render' myself! What does that even mean? Who speaks like that?"

"Even as I say, it doesn't mean any*one* does."

"Because you're no one."

"Because I am you, and as you are now… that's right, I am no one."

CHAPTER 25

Your cousin taught your grandma how to send voice notes with her phone, and not a minute passed before she sent you this bit:

You know, *lijo,* I was thinking of our last conversation, when you were on watch on the bridge, and it's nice that you work on ships. I've been on boats riding up the rivers up to Pasiga but nothing more than that. To think you have crossed oceans and it's no metaphor!

What a career you picked!

But I know you were lazy.

Don't think I don't know.

You went for that profession because your dad does it and you figured he's doing well for himself financially so why shouldn't you? It's not like we're full of options here in Panama anyway. Not that you knew what you wanted back then nor would you have dared to go for it if you had. You made your choice and here you are. Or you are there. And I haven't seen you in a year. But that's okay.

I know you're well.

When I first saw the ocean it wasn't as dramatic as you'd think. I didn't mention it to the Willoughby's. I was carrying the groceries up the pathway to their house when I heard the far-off crashing of the waves, the up and down, the salty tones that lingered in the air. That settled on my tongue.

I didn't get to see the ocean fully until after sunset, when the job was done. I asked if I could go for a walk in the sand. I got a nod.

I went.

I was dumb enough to wear shoes and socks, because why not? That's what one wears to go for walks, right?

I saw my feet dig my weight into the ground. I took them off. The grains of sand clung onto my skin, between my toes. It was cold. Dark. There was no moon; and the ocean was so black I couldn't tell it from the sky.

I was sad I didn't get to see it during the day. But tell me, *lijo,* since you've been out there*:* Does it feel any less grand when it's blue instead of black?

***

I remember how I felt. The memory is vivid.

When the sun rose, everyone was asleep. The night before, they told me they'd go for brunch later in the morning, which I learned is a thing they do on Sundays because they don't want to wake up for breakfast. Imagine waking up to eat being a burden and not a privilege: one time *Señora* asked me to *remind* her to drink water!

In any case, it was good they slept in because I had the whole morning to see the ocean when it was blue. It was early. Sunrise hadn't finished tincturing the sky. The water was still dark, but there were other colors: tiny glitters of sun sparkled in the light, the cool breeze of dawn combing the wavelets into white. Crashing against the black sand. I thought it'd be white, or at least lighter in color, but it was as black as the night I'd hoped would end so I could see the beach.

Not all of it was black, though. There were gashes of white sand and shiny seashells speckling the black. The closer I looked the more I noticed the ratio of black against the white: a dark background flecked in white scatterings with the occasional colorful seashell.

And I know.

You can probably figure out what I'm getting at, but it's true. That is how I felt. As clichéd as it may sound. The white sand looked like stars shining in the sky. As if the starlit dome had melted from above and plastered on the ground. I was walking *on* the night, looking at the day.

Even after all these years, the memory is lush, alive in un-blemished detail, and I wonder how something so far in the past can be summoned with such verve, with such meticulous recall I can feel the sand under my feet.

It makes me sad.

It makes me sad because it was the *one* happy moment of my childhood. And how is it not sad to call what I lived child-hood? I was an employee, and children don't have jobs. They shouldn't, at least.

So when did my childhood end? Was it when I became a whore or when I became a maid?

When did I become an adult?

Does getting paid make you an adult? Because it's the only correlation I can find between the two. Is it the loneliness?

Is it the silence?

***

I remember it was Monday.

Most people had gone back to the city to carry on with their jobs. The Willoughbys had a long weekend, however, which meant Will didn't have to go to work on Monday.

We stayed.

The beach was practically empty during the weekdays. Nobody showed up before noon. With the city people gone, the locals got to enjoy the beach. They had five days without the *jefes*, and the *yeyesitos* (rich people), and they'd make the best of it. Some of them even lived in their employers' homes while they were gone.

I remember you told me the entire place was like Feudal Japan, where the *daimyos* owned the land but allowed the peas-ants to live there. These had a nicer life than the rest, which had to keep an apartment or a house of their own far away. They were honest people, though. Years of trust. Nobody set foot in these houses other than those to whom they'd been entrusted. Still, the workers flaunted their fancy housing as if it were theirs. Semantics, in the end, was all that prevented them from saying they 'lived' there.

Five days out of seven, most weeks out of the year except for summer and the holidays in November, it was at least seventy percent of the year that they lived in those houses without their bosses in them, and that's *if* they went every weekend, which they didn't.

The city was a good two-hour drive, and in a country where people are only used to drive short distances on cratered roads, two hours is considered *metido* – deep in there: Far away.

My bosses were still in town, and on that day I was allowed to sit with them on the sand. I left early.

They said they needed to finish a phone call and they'd come and join me. I brought the food, the beach blanket, and set up the umbrella. I took the liberty to drink one of the juice packets.

It was a nice day. Sunny. Faint breeze. There was no music playing. No kids were running around.

The sand, untouched.

On the weekends, when the city people are there, ATV tracks dig into the sand. They race each other and drive along the coast.

But when they're gone, all you can see are footprints and horse hooves.

None of the locals owned an ATV.

What for?

You can't take it on the road, even if you could get away with driving it to town, though it's not likely, what's the point?

Luxury, or entertainment, which is itself a luxury: like myself.

I was looking at the waves when I heard someone calling from behind me. "*Mami! Mami!*"

It was a man's voice. And the tone was clear.

Mami in this context doesn't mean 'Mommy,' it means something like 'shortie' or 'hot stuff.'

I wasn't even wearing a swimsuit – and look at where my

mind goes! - as if *that* would make it acceptable. As if me wearing a swimsuit would make it fine! But what could I expect, right? We can't blame the dog for biting when you're a piece of meat, right?

No. It's *my* damn fault. Always!

I'm sorry, *lijo.*

It makes me angry to remember.

Anyway, I was wearing shorts and a T-shirt. But I had forgotten. These cute little days of walking on the beach and sleeping on a nice bed and eating good food... I forgot myself: who did I think I was feeling all content?

How could they *not* call me out?

How could they *not* assume I'd make myself available when called?

To these men, I'm just another whore they are entitled to, but I had not realized this yet.

Not back then.

At first I thought they knew my uncle, or my father. I turned around because I thought perhaps I'd know them, but my curiosity looked like consent to them, and by responding to their call I confirmed I was a whore.

Their eyes lit up, and why wouldn't they? They called out into the air for a piece of ass and I responded. My placid gaze and patient eyes may as well have pulled them between my legs.

This was the lesson of the day.

In their minds, attention means permission.

They walked over.

There were three of them. They stood in a triangle shape with the tallest one in the middle, the apex, and two squirrelly, stumpy men behind him acting as his vertices: a douchebag isosceles.

"Mami, que paso? 'Tas solita?" he said - "Hot stuff, what happened? You on your own?" - as if he had to save me from my solitude; as if he wasn't what I should be safe from in the first

place.

Lucky for me, a familiar voice called from afar.

"Rin!" said Mr. Willoughby, family in tow.

"Mr. Willoughby!" I said, ashamed, like it was my fault these men were so close to our picnic.

"Who are you people?" Mr. Willoughby asked them. "Why are you bothering my daughter? Go away."

I can't remember the exact words, but he did say 'daughter.'

The men laughed and said, *"Nos vemos, bastardita,"* and left.

Mr. Willoughby meant well by calling me his daughter. They were a kind family. But the Willoughby's were blonde, white-skinned, and blue-eyed – the sun, the clouds, and the sky depicted on their faces - and I wasn't.

When a man like Mr. Willoughby calls me his daughter, with his family standing right next to him, everybody thinks I'm a bastard. And when you're a bastard, everybody calls your mother a whore.

My dead mother, degraded like this.

Again, I was amazed at what some men would try with a gaze: they would turn a dead woman into a whore, as easily as her little girl.

The Willoughby's sat next to me and opened up the cooler. They packed beers and juices and snacks for the afternoon. They even brought a towel for me. It was nice. The water was warm, too, and the wind had died down.

I got dirty looks from workers on the beach, accusatory looks, as if I were some sort of traitor for not sunning with 'my kind.'

It wasn't only about money.

It was also about race.

Class, and caste.

CHAPTER 26

Every day had been sunny since you arrived at the hotel.

The window only opened about six inches from the sill, a bit less than a hand's length, enough for air but not for wind. The management said it was for the pigeons and the seagulls: "they'd fly into the room and rarely come out alive. Feisty fuckers, too."

You thought about your grandmother's story, about your grandfather and what he'd done, or not done, you thought about other stories you've heard from friends and people from the ship, and you saw the pattern.

How come people from different backgrounds, upbringing, cultures, and levels of education, could fall prey to, as you said, *the same shit*? And the thing is, Orlando, we're rarely original in our vices; we can only be unique in virtue.

Only in the good, not the bad, do we find originality.

And I'll repeat what your grandmother told you back when you asked her why you kept doing the same shit even when you knew it's wasn't right.

"It's like this, *lijo*," she said to you. "Knowing better doesn't mean you'll do your best. Every passion cries for what it lacks. Be happy inside, lack nothing, and good will come."

It sounded simple in her voice, and perhaps it was simple. But simple rarely means easy, and this was no exception.

There's being unique and there's being original.

And people aren't as unique as they think. Social media has done away with this perceived uniqueness. Before, if you felt different from those around you, that was it. You lived with either the pride or the shame of being an outcast, but you can find someone like you, like-minded, all the way out in Japan, or Norway, India, or New Zealand.

I know it feels good to be unique, but it feels great to nurture uniqueness as a collective.

This is what originality is.

You didn't get it at first and even shrugged it off as sappy, but it made sense to you in that room. Every day you woke up to keep your journal and then engorged yourself self-help online. But you retained nothing.

What did you think was going to happen? You think you'd wake up one day and shit would be fine?

All these things you read and write amount to no more than a hand extended: it will assist, sure, it'll stabilize you as you stand up, but you've got to plant your feet on the ground and push up. Otherwise, you'll keep doing *the same shit* even when you know better and all that does is kick you on the teeth as you linger on the ground telling yourself you're looking at the sky.

Bullshit you are.

***

Do you remember your trip to China?

Not the one after high school, but the one when you were about fifteen years old.

If it's a blur it's because it was for most of the time. The rare occasions where you could've mustered a unique experience, you didn't. You chose obscurity, ennui, and jerking off four to six times a day to make yourself sleep through it all.

And it's easy to reprimand yourself, "Oh, had I known then what I know now; I could've done this or that; such a waste..." but you weren't who you are now, not then. So what's the point?

The circumstances where different, mentally more so than physically. You were a child, afraid, dependent on the approval not only of your parents but of the people in whose care you were entrusted. You experienced so much culture, inadvertently, so much authenticity despite your looking the other way, and thinking back on it you can't help but be grateful the memories have lingered and spark in you a desire to revisit them, now, as you are, after so many years, finally: curious.

It was a small urban town about an hour away from Guangzhou. When you compare it to the towns you were used to seeing in Panama, Hua Du was a city in itself, though they kept calling it a 'town.'

Our connection was a lot fainter back then, practically non-existent, but I was there as much as you were, and just as dissociated.

Huadu is one of the eleven urban districts forming part of the city of Guangzhou, capital of the Guangdong Province, China, of which you didn't know shit, but this is where you were.

You soon learned of the various dialects people spoke, including the common-tongue, Mandarin, and were immediately drawn to how they could all speak three to four dialects plus Mandarin and Spanish and even some English to boot.

There were shops e.v.e.r.y.w.h.e.re. and throngs of people hawking stuff in the street and food-stands and a million necks turning as you passed wondering how the fuck were you born with eyes like that.

People stared.

They approached you and stood in front of you and stared as if you were an inanimate object on display. You knew it was because you were different, peculiar in their eyes *because* of your eyes.

The dynamics of your lodging are irrelevant now because it isn't what has lingered in your mind. It isn't what has shaped in you that need for exploration. In any case, much of your attitude toward travel and 'living on the horizon' stems from the time you spent in the 'little' town of Huadu.

When you first heard the name of the town, it was pronounced *Fah-too*, which you later learned was how the locals referred to it in the Cantonese and Hakka dialects. It was your understanding that neither Cantonese nor Hakka had standardized writing, as opposed to Mandarin, which in turn made them both dialects and not a language. But what's it to you now? All this knowledge of the language and its etymology. Why do you give a fuck now? To pretend you've been paying attention?

But you haven't.

You didn't.

And there's no getting around it.

That whole trip is proof of your outrageous knack for dissociation, a knack you honed into a skill over which you now have no control.

It takes over.

It takes you way inside your head and you lose your mind within itself. The 'ruling reason' you read about in Stoic books finds itself unfettered and flailing about in a cage without a will, and it was there that we found each other.

It was there, that I floated from the oblivion that is your lack of self: a hole with the right vacuity and lowered pressure to drag me into your side of consciousness, to grant me an identity of my own. And here we are: two in one – and yet not, because we could as well be one in two – who knows?

Not us, for sure.

I remember your time in China because it's when I got my first peek into your side of things. Your side of *us.*

At first, it was as if through keyholes: fleeting glimpses and far-cries of the environment you perceived around yourself. And because I had no spectrum of sensation to feel things for myself, all I knew about the world were the frames you filtered through your dens of bias. When you were happy, which often meant well-fed, the world I saw smelled and sounded like billowing roses with clouds instead of thorns and all ranges of delectable flavors. But when you weren't, I saw blood where smiles should be and heard croaks instead of songs. There was no middle-ground for you. All you gave me was the best and the worst of it. And I could do nothing but live in a swamp of shit and roses.

I asked you the other day what you remembered from Huadu and you said, "I remember the supermarket."

It's always about food with you.

"I remember the second floor had a bunch of dried sausages I could never take a liking to," you said, "and the first floor had DVDs of Dragon Ball GT in Mandarin. I watched all of it. In Mandarin. Understanding nothing. That's how bored I was."

You did remember the park. You remember the streets and you can probably still find your way around the city. You've always been good with finding your bearings. This much I'll give you.

It'd take you one go around, no matter how far you went, to map out the whole place in your head. You could find your way back to where you came and then do it all the next day as if you'd been commuting on those streets your entire life.

Why is that, you wonder? Defense.

Because you're lost enough inside, your instinct keeps you from getting lost outside.

Bullshit, you say?

Not at all.

What the fuck do you know about being you?

You haven't been watching, but I have.

Anyway...

The street and back-alleys were your favorite haunts. You loved how narrow they were and the array of smells you caught gusting like wind into a valley.

Small spaces entice you: "the smaller the space the more of it I own," you said to me once, "the more of it I occupy."

I still don't get it, but good on you. The point is: you'd spend most of your outings in these alleys and you're lucky nobody fucked with you and the locals left you alone. The places you walked around in weren't exactly safe, and yet you never felt in danger. You were used to the staring, so you thought it normal when people followed you with their eyes and looked at you from their windows. You didn't mind when they shouted because you didn't know what they were saying, and they shouted more often than they spoke so what difference did it make?

They could as well have been threatening you, but if you didn't know and you kept coming back every day, I suppose they must've thought you brave. Perhaps dangerous. And you began to correlate a lack of interest as a quality worthy of respect. You even saw it in anime, which confirmed your opinion, where some characters who were perceived to be cool were presented as unimpressionable and nonchalant.

It was from these faint, imperceptible inputs that you gleaned most of the filters I talked about earlier, and so when you spoke with people or gathered new experiences, you'd sift the memories through these filters and come out with a bastardized picture of what happened.

And everyone does this.

It's human.

Plato wrote about it in his theory of Ideal Forms, where he says that everything has an ideal form of which we perceive but a shadow.

There are as many worlds as there are minds to perceive them.

But, I know: digression...

There was a particular alley you liked around the corner of the building where you stayed. There were food-stands all along the alley and people selling fruits and snacks and boiled sweet potatoes. There was a baker you always went to for *boluo bao,* a round and puffy piece of bread frosted with pineapple-flavored sugar. And you fucking *loved* that shit. Ate like six of them a day. At least! Skipped jerk-off sessions to go out and get more.

Now you wouldn't even think of eating one of those, let alone six.

Further down the alley around another corner was the main street with a huge plaza at the center. You'd always pinpoint it because there was a leather store off to the side, and it had a rose on the logo. I think this is why the images I saw of what *you* saw were focused on red roses. Not only did you see it every day, but it made you feel – in your fucked up head – immeasurably sad and alone.

In truth, though, you were bored.

And your mind cannot handle boredom. I bet this is news to you, too, though it shouldn't be. Don't feel too bad. Think of what Nietzsche wrote, "Against boredom, even God struggles in vain."

And like a god would, you made 'mountains out of molehills' to keep yourself entertained, even if the worst was yet to come. The hallucinations you let your madness squeeze into your brain – the tale of how you murdered someone in an alley – became troublesome, and categorically so.

But of that later.

CHAPTER 27

It must've been the ninth day, or somewhere around that time, past the first week and before the next, when you had a nightmare about your mother.

You used to have them all the time in college; and even when you had a place of your own with someone next to you in bed, you still screamed out the anger you had suppressed as a child.

But we've addressed this.

You remember all the shit but none of the good and it makes sense because the smell of rot is stronger than any fragrance and yet – it's fair to note this, so listen up – your mother always encouraged you to greatness.

Whether you owe it to her or you owe it to yourself she never specified, but fact remains: given the privilege they had worked hard to prop you into, it's not unreasonable of them to hope you'd be aiming at stars instead of hills.

Your grandmother told you to never feel guilty for being fortunate. It helps no one and dishonors the hard work your family put in to get you there.

"As long as you are grateful and humble," she said, "you've earned your fortune."

So, the nightmares.

They'd always be about an imagined fight with undertones of ones that did happen. I won't enumerate the fights or the *correazos* because they would shed a bad light on your mother, and it'd be way out of context.

Yes, you got spanked, to use a word, and yes, you were

grounded, and yes, thinking back there were many things she could've done better to handle all the shit she fed into your mind and all the storms she made your heart leak inside your head, but seriously, man – I'm telling you - you came out of nowhere.

She had no idea what to do. She was twenty-three. Fending for herself! What the fuck did you know at twenty-three?

Your relationship with your mother wasn't the best. And she'd argue there were worse parents than her and at least she didn't burn any cigarettes on your eyelids or gave you away like her grandfather did to her mother. But shit's simple: if it is like Voltaire wrote and 'we live in the best of all possible worlds,' then your mother was the best mother you could've had because anyone else wouldn't have cut it.

You weren't a great son, either, and your arguments as to how there are worse sons than you is as bland as any platitude, as insubstantial as her excuses, because you needed each other. Even if you did bring out the worse in each other, like all people who are tethered by love, like any family who is 'unhappy in its own way' but gets stronger as it heals.

But!

Even if your relationship with your mother had its hurdles, it has improved as you have both grown into something more compatible. You've become more understanding. You've seen parenthood for yourself now.

And your mother lost her stringency with age, because grandmothers would much rather be loved than obeyed.

Your grandmother is perfect proof. Your mother said your grandmother used to be mean but you can't picture it. She is so calm now. So soothing. But it could well be true. After all, virtue isn't loud. In nature, the wildest storms are advertised and followed by ponderous silence. Thunder thinks itself a whisper. Lightning knows it's but a flicker smothered by the stars.

Your grandmother, too, isn't loud anymore. To you, she was as faint, yet as expressive, as cathartic, as a sigh. And maybe your mother can be for your daughter what your grandmother was to you.

Still, regardless of this possibility, you remember the verbal abuse: her insults searing into your skin until they looked like birth marks, as if they were there all along. As if they were true.

And you believed in them.

You believed you were the trash you were accused of being. And why couldn't she hate your father instead of you, you wonder? Because when you can't afford to hate the man who puts a burden on your back, you hate the burden instead. The child.

You.

And it wasn't much better with your father. You can't even remember the last time you had an actual conversation that didn't turn into a session in which he spoke about himself or preached on what you should do, giving you a long list of terrible scenarios of what would happen if you don't do things as he suggested and if one of those terrible scenarios were to happen, he'd be the first to tell you he told you so.

And why don't you get along?

Was it the constant mockery?

The condescension?

The lack of respect and the cultural assurance that parents aren't supposed to respect their children?

But have you considered if what you thought was condescension was, instead, *concern*? The perpetual worry that you'd suffer even the slightest discomfort? Because even if you're thirty years old and have a child of your own, he feels the need to review how to turn on the car lights before you go.

Because he won't admit to you he's worried.

He won't say it pains him to see you drive off on your own.

Still, after all this time, "Always."

He won't tell you but you *understand* - the outright terror, the sheer horror - to outlive a child… no amount of pain is worse; and he would not forgive himself if you crashed in the split second it took for you to find the light switch on your own.

So give him a break.

You'll never forget when he scoffed at the short story you gave him when you were nine years old. It hurt you because you made that and you'd shown it to him first. It was a parody of *The Legend of Zelda: Ocarina of Time,* and you even bound it in *Deku*-green construction paper. It hurt you, and you later wondered if your aspiration had been stronger maybe he would've believed in it – but *fuck that, fuck him* - or better yet: you wouldn't have cared if he cared, which was best.

You keep the memory because it proves your love of writing from an early age.

And it feels good. It validates you.

It grants your dream a pedigree.

It proves it's not a passing fancy but a long-yearned want.

It makes it passion.

But why didn't you get along? Perhaps it was because you adopted the worse of his qualities and none of the good. Because he exercised his best qualities at work and not at home, which is why you only learned to look up to him when you joined him in the profession.

You clash because you find in him all the things you hate about yourself, and he resents that you pride yourself in qualities that had nothing to do with him.

Still, in time things improved.

If your relationship with your mother was comprised of rage and screams, the one with your father was mostly silence and aversion. Silence and aversion, then, was the attitude you adopted for the entirety of your teenage years. Until you left.

Until you were happy.

You must understand they were raised in a culture where communal acceptance is more important than self-acceptance, and when a child is different from the norm he migrates to a world where parents can't help him because they're out of their element.

Even if it's similar in technique, a bird can't teach a turtle how to swim.

The details of the 'falling-out' don't matter. What matters is you're still resentful. Even if your relationship with him has also improved, you still go back to the argument and think of how it wasn't resolved, that time merely passed and you both figured you'd let it go, which was strange because he never let shit go.

He loves being right, you always said. *He loves saying 'I told you so' more than he loves anything else. More than he loved me.*

"But he was in the wrong," you insisted.

"It doesn't matter anymore," I said. "What matters is he thought he was right, he was hurt, and he still moved past it. And so should you."

You've got to let that go.

Both of you.

Because it's tough for a father-son relationship to hold as it is, and even more so when you're polar opposites.

It is no news to you, or him, that your relationship is a struggle. But the problem never was your nature. It was your choice to shut yourself out.

You denied your father the chance to step up and listen, to make an effort. When you allow yourself to speak true, whatever the result it would at least be an honest one, but you repressed, and he took your silence as agreement when it wasn't even a concession: because *you* gave up on *him*.

You gave up on him ever being able to understand. You thought he was too conditioned and way past being someone you could objectively respect as a person, and you left. You left long before he was even tempted to give up on you and then when his time did come: he didn't.

He's not perfect. And he never will be. Neither will you. But if you allow yourselves to be, you can both be good.

And that is enough.

You know parenting is tough.

You've learned it with your daughter.

You've seen it in books and film.

How come practically every hero is an orphan?

Is it because good parenting lies in the mythical balance of 'being there' and staying the fuck out of the way?

If so, you'll always make mistakes: because even if some parents manage the former, no good parent can possibly achieve the latter.

But as long as your failures are *yours*, and not the same as your parents', you'll fail *forward*, which is a win.

You've learned progressive parenthood isn't about perfection, but about making new mistakes, finding new solutions, and to cease the perpetuation of trauma, of old mistakes, and to stop insecurities from being hereditary.

It's okay to make mistakes as long as they are new ones, as long as they're admitted as such, and as long as you take fruitful action.

It's hard work.

And all that rhetoric about children being invariably a blessing... well, that's some bullshit, too.

It *is* hard to love them sometimes, and it's okay to say it.

It'd be a lie to say otherwise, even if it's a lie everyone tells themselves, a lie they tell to each other, and even as they do it they *know* it's but a vicious lie masked with piousness and diligence, even as they nod to each other in agreement of their lie because it'd be oh, so blasphemous to admit loving a child is hard.

But *you* don't lie to yourself about it.

It's okay to be mad.

You can be mad at her, and she can be mad at you.

Feelings are real and pretending they are not didn't work out well for you growing up.

But you *are* grateful for her.

Children: they seem weak but they're strong enough to

break your heart.

She made you feel when you thought you were all dried up, when you thought you had felt all you could physically feel.

And no, she didn't give you a purpose.

That's another lie.

A pernicious one, too, because it burdens the child with the expectation of bringing gratification, and fuck that, too.

She made you see you could, and should, be better.

That you had to make yourself happy first.

Better.

You love her for who she has spurred you to be.

And you love who you've become for her sake, because you sure as shit wouldn't have done it for yours.

You like yourself when you're with her, and it's about time you did, because you've hated yourself too long.

***

"Aren't you excited to go back onboard?" I asked you. "A change."

Your sighs had become laden, more and more as the days went by, and though a sigh is by definition an exhale, you didn't let anything out.

"A change, yes," you said, in the tone I've learned precedes a long tirade of admonishments and negativity, "I guess."

But you didn't do any of that. Instead, you were in one of those moods where I need to poke and poke until you speak.

I poked.

"So what's the problem now?" I asked.

"Same shit."

"You know shit dries eventually. Stops stinking, too."

"Not this shit."

"Not if you keep watering it to keep it moist."

"Is this supposed to be clever? It's disgusting."

"It's funny, though."

And it did make you blow out a chuckle into the air. Poop is always funny. Done. We could talk now.

"I remember when I thought going out to sea would be

cool," you said. "I thought it'd be like all the lofty things I read on 'being a part of something larger' and all that shit."

"But no?"

"But no," you went on, "most people I've met onboard don't look ahead to be humbled by something larger, instead they look behind to feel enlarged by lording over something smaller. They have power but no authority. They can say No but rarely Yes. Onboard, you can use power to say No, but to say Yes you need authority, and because they don't have it they latch on to petty matters to exercise their pent-up power and brittle egos. It's annoying and, what's worse, predictable because more often than not you don't meet people but archetypes of people: a type, not an individual."

You did go on for a tirade…

"And you never did this?" I poked some more.

"At times, yes. I did it, too. I did a lot of shit I always told myself I'd never do. Acted in ways I told myself I'd never act. All that. I thought I was a good person but I just hadn't had the chance to be bad."

"Which makes a world of difference."

"Yeah," you said, stood up and did some pushups to wake up, "I also went around saying I didn't need anyone, that I was as self-sufficient as I was smart and I could bear all of it on my own. All of it."

"But no?"

"But no. I only thought that because the challenges I had faced could all be conquered with one hand. It was less than luck. It was privilege. Indifferent chaos with the stability of a cloud. I built lavish forts to keep me safe, but they soon dissipated like they were never there."

"What dissipated? The privilege?"

"The ignorance of it."

"The ignorance of privilege?"

"Yes, like being sheltered."

"Right."

"Right," you said as you sat by the laptop. "Speaking of

which, perhaps I should go on writing. My grandmother was at the beach and not even one hour went by before someone called her a bastard."

"Go on."

CHAPTER 28

"Bastardita," she whispered to herself, slight laugh, faint smile. "Can you believe it, *lijo*?"

"I'm sorry," you told her.

"Ay, *lijo*," she smiled, her cheeks bearing the weight of all her heartbreaks, "what to do."

My mother had been dead all my life, *lijo*, and I didn't know much about her life other than she was married to my dad - before they had me - so how could I be a bastard? It made me angry because the whole time I'd been with the Willoughbys I felt good about myself. I had a job and I was appreciated for it. It was comfortable and honest and I was beginning to feel proud of myself.

Ay, *lijo*, the other day you sounded sad over the phone, but it may bring you some comfort to know we're never less alone than we're sad. But sadly, the reverse is just as true.

This is exactly when people lash out at you, when you begin to be happy with yourself – it's like they smell your satisfaction – and they move in with criticism and negativity.

The men left and all the other ones running around the beach left as well, as if the Willoughbys' presence made them wary of what they would say to their bosses next weekend. Will was carrying a small cooler, and *Señora* had a couple of bottles of cold, white wine to sip on under the sun. I wondered why the bottles weren't in the cooler.

They brought more towels and an extra umbrella so we had more space to spread, and a small portable radio to listen to the game, whatever game it was.

Then it was quiet.

It was nice.

The breeze was cool and not strong enough to blow the umbrellas away, which was nice.

The morning went by quietly. *Señora* was passed out under her umbrella after her fourth glass of wine and what little remained in the bottle dripped out slowly, reflecting the bright rays of noon and darkening the sand.

The kids were playing in the water. Meanwhile, Will was busy figuring out how to tell me they were moving out of Panama. I know this now, but I didn't then. He said nothing of it. Instead, he told me I could go on vacation for the holidays if I wanted.

I said, "Sure."

I missed my sister.

***

It took me an innumerable amount of bus rides and transfers to get back to my hometown.

I didn't remember it taking so long to get out, but maybe it was because back then every step away from that place came with a feeling of relief. But now, I was filled with worry and a good amount of dread.

I wanted to see my sister but I wasn't keen on reliving all those terrible memories. I could only hope she'd have no bad memories to trade with mine.

When I finally arrived, I looked around and it all looked so beautiful. The mountains and sloping fields of corn and vast, grazing pastures, the cows chilling about, the horses galloping all over the place with manes flying: it was beautiful. I almost missed it. I almost wanted to go back. But I put away the thought.

My sister was a lot taller than I remembered her, and her voice was deeper, older, but what was best: it was cheery, had a skip to it. She had smile on her face and the confidence to shout out my name as she ran to me. I knew it was a good idea to have left.

I was made to be a weed, and she was a flower.

I could tell she had bloomed.

And it made me happy.

The Willoughbys had given me an advanced payment for the holidays, but since I didn't go anywhere when I was in the city, I never spent anything. I was flush. I had all my money in my pockets. I could buy her all the things she wanted. Clothes, snacks, whatever. Things were different now. We didn't need anyone. Not our father and not our aunts. We certainly didn't need anyone's unwanted patronage on a parking lot. Yes, things were different. *I* was different.

We went for a walk by the river where we used to pick up water. It was nice to watch the water go by. To enjoy and not have to fill up heavy buckets to carry them back.

"How is the city?" she asked me. "I heard the buildings are tall."

I wanted to tell her everything. All the amazing things I saw. The cars. The trucks. The roads and motorcycles and refrigerators and stoves and televisions. Radios. Planes. The beach. The ocean! Everything! But I paced myself.

I didn't want her to think I was happy to have left her behind. She didn't say anything, nor would she, but I could tell part of her resented me for leaving. Part of her was grateful, though, because she knows she would've been called a whore by association. I could picture them shouting out, "*Las putihermanas!*"

Sister whores! Sister whores!

I said the city was hard work, but that I liked it. She told me she was going to school, that she made lots of friends, and how everyone thought she was cute and nobody thought she was a whore because of it.

"I remember why you left," she told me. "I know why you stayed away."

I liked to see her this confident, this exacting with her

words, and all assertive in intent. School, socializing: it was doing her good. And all was well.

"I had to," I said, "it was for the best."

"I still missed you."

"I missed you too."

"Will you *please* tell me about the city now?"

She knew I was holding back. I miss this. Her, yes, but this the most: being understood, despite my silence; being understood, despite my hiding away. It felt good. The Willoughbys were good to me in the sense that they didn't reject me and didn't make me feel like I was less, but my sister, Adema, was good *for* me because she made me feel embraced and I didn't know I needed that. And I hoped I did the same for her, or, even better, that she didn't need to be embraced at all.

Later that afternoon, I bought us some sodas from the store and went back to the river. It hadn't rained in a while, so the water was kind of warm and there was no danger of a surge. It felt nice to pay for sodas in the same shop which some time ago had denied us bread. They can't deny me service if I have money. Honest-earned money. They didn't recognize me at first, Adema later told me, and she thought it odd because she said I looked the same.

But I didn't. Not quite.

Back then, they weren't looking at my face but at my expression. I used to be scared and shy, but this time I wasn't ashamed to be myself. I was proud. And it was this they didn't recognize. They didn't like it either, because when people look down on you your confidence looks like insolence to them. Your silence and composure speaks of a world that is your own, all within yourself, one where they're not invited, and they feel left out. They hate you because they think you're conceited, but when it's confidence and not false pomp, not insolence, you don't care either way, and you do as you would. As I did.

I was happy to see my sister, and when I saw her go to school all dressed up in her uniform and a backpack filled with books, a smile so laced with hope, her eyes bright and in love with it all, I was proud of her too. I told her I'd go to the river while I waited for her. I had brought my Bible, which I had got into the habit of reading. I liked the stories.

It was walking back from the river, on my way to pick up Adema, that I met your grandfather.

***

He was taller than the other boys, particularly riding his horse as I stomped about on my short, choppy legs.

See? There's self-criticism again.

Even remembering the times where he thought me desirable make me cringe. I wonder if men want us only for the brief moment we don't want them back, to see themselves wanted so they can leave with their pride while we stay with our wanting.

I don't know, *lijo*.

I don't often reflect on these things but telling you my story makes room for introspection. I'd always taken the pain as due diligence, never asking myself if there was any sense to it, or whether or not I deserved it. Anyway... he was tall, handsome, and the sun behind his back gave him an air of grandness.

I was smitten.

I walked past him and he said, "Hey, where are off to looking so cute?"

At that age I thought it was a nice thing to say. But with what I'd seen of some men back then, back there, you'd think I would've known better. You'd think I would've known he used this phrase a million times before, that it had worked many times and so he used it as a lure instead of genuine praise. I should've known he didn't see me as an individual, that I was no more than target-practice for his ego.

You'd think I would've noticed he didn't even stop his horse to say it, as if it were my job to follow him with my eyes instead of him stopping to meet mine. I'm ashamed to admit I was 'one of those girls' who fell for a cheap, pick-up phrase. And I should've known then – *had* I known then! – that this foreshadowed he'd never stop moving for me, because even years later, as it was on that day, I was no more than a passing fancy.

CHAPTER 29

The more you write about your grandmother the more I remember the things she said to you as a child.

You do it with your daughter, too, saying things to her that are meant for yourself, but they're easier to assimilate when said to someone else. I'm sure there's a psychological term for it, though I don't know it and you certainly don't either. Perhaps it's the same thing as journaling.

You were riding on your horse and she was pulling him by the reigns. You were too young to ride on your own and your horse grew a lot faster than you had. Seeing you looking down on her from a moving horse must've stirred some memories in her. She did always say you looked like your grandfather. Maybe that's why she loves you so much. Maybe that's why she spoils you. She figured a grandson is bound to leave her, so at least you were honest from the start.

There was a girl you liked – you must've been in second grade – but the girl didn't like you back, or at least you didn't know. Even now you remember her denim jacket cradling her shiny brown locks as she walked around the classroom, her freckles mustered on her cheeks as she smiled at nothing, or everything, though certainly not at you. A pink red flower on the jacket.

You had moved to her school, the classroom was at the end of the hall. This you remember in vivid detail. Your brain is wired for exploration and route-recall. Again, I'm sure there are psychological terms for this, but I don't know them. The point is: you're good at remembering places and mapping them out in your mind and always find your way in or out of them, and yet this is not so for your emotional pathways.

Anyway: the girl.

It was a breezy day. You liked her but it was unrequited. You passed the store on the left and kept to the sidewalk. You were on a horse, which is common in your grandmother's town. You remember the sound of her *chancletas* sliding against the concrete, flip-and-flopping, the cheap pink plastic digging into her skin. You remember that sound hustling around the kitchen, the yard, late at night when you were sleeping. Over the years there was less flip-and-flopping and more dragging, the soles as smooth as glass, and just as brittle. Perhaps her legs were tired. Perhaps her heart.

She looked ahead at the bare sidewalk, then looked at you, and said, "You know, *lijo*, when you feel unloved, or those you care for have done you wrong, it's not unhealthy to love yourself entirely out of spite."

And your situation did not warrant that response. It was puppy-love at best. And not even that. But she knew better than to dismiss the sting of unrequited love, regardless of its validity or its comparative burden to what she'd experienced. She knew better than to shrug it off, and so she didn't. Your world was small, Orlando, and so it was natural your problems were also small. She understood that, but she gave you a response as heavy as the emotions you were feeling. She didn't belittle your situation or your concerns, and as a child, this was rare, because everything anyone ever told you was to be grateful your problems were so small, because they would only get worse, yet nobody ever helped you overcome them. So when the so-called bigger problems came, you weren't ready. You were ill-equipped. Your grandmother wasn't like that. And though you don't remember her words, you remember feeling heard. Acknowledged. And that feeling is marked deep inside yourself. You didn't need some grand gesture, all you wanted was for someone to be quiet while you spoke, to listen to you, even if you *were* a child.

And for the first time, even if it wasn't the first time: You remember feeling loved, and loving back.

***

You used to be afraid of the dark.

This was another thing your grandmother dispelled. She had a plot of land in Pasiga, a county in Panama's Chiman District established in 1998 with a population of a little over four hundred people.

Your images of the place come in flashes: a steady strobe of memory paired with the occasional flash of stories your grandmother told you. To bring the events back to the surface, I'll need to quickly list them: the mother-pig chasing after you, chasing river shrimp as you swam around the rocks, grabbing *cherele* snails and cooking them in garlic and oil; the calf kicking your face, herding cattle on a horse with your uncle and cousin, sprinkling soil on corn dough to make crunchier *tortilla* sticks. And your grandmother pretending she didn't notice.

The green fields, the hills, the wooden house thrown together with a room and a bed. The mud-and-clay kitchen off to the side, the small porch where your cousins and sisters choreographed a dance for the local kids.

Is it all coming back?

See?

I'll keep going.

How about the time when you were all gathered by the bull pens, sitting on the railings watching your uncles wrestle the calves to the ground?

You were terrified of touching them. You have a faint memory of getting kicked in the face by one of them, and though your grandmother keeps telling you there is no way that happened because your face would be disfigured, you retain the image of a hoof approaching and, like in many a future instance, you grandmother was trying to assuage a growing trauma… like the one you had of the dark.

I'm sure if you went to a therapist you'd find out the source of it. I mean, it's not like it's uncommon, though the causality may be particular to you. In any case, you're presently not afraid of cows or pigs, so she took away those fears, but the darkness took a while.

Do you remember being on the boat with her? This part you remember. I know because you dreamt of it the other day. You remember the fishing harbor from where you boarded the small open-decked wooden boat, laden with around ten to twelve people bunched up with totes of clothing and bags of rice. The harbor could've been around an hour from *La Mesa*, though you have no memory of the ride there. You remember feeling on the edge of the world, and not because the world had ended, but because it had transcended what you knew. You grew up in the city, surrounded by buildings and cars and people dressed in nice clothes. Even at your grandmother's house people went about their days and you never saw anyone laboring because you only went during the weekends.

But here at the wharf, the bustle struck you as other-worldly. Because to you, it was indeed beyond the world you knew: the world in which your parents had grown was foreign to your sheltered mind. Perhaps this is why they encouraged you to spend time with your grandmother. The more you think of it, the more you see the effect that spending time with her had on your personality.

You mostly remember the cement. The mossy overgrowth along the ramp leading to the water. There was a restaurant off the side. In your mind, the images are steady in setting but distorted in time. You faced an empty parking lot: a kiosk selling sodas and some of those sweet cookies you remember from your lunch boxes. *Galletas del bus.* They used to come in a carton shaped like a school bus. Your favorite was lemon flavor.

You dwell on the nostalgia but you would never eat that much sugar nowadays. You're not sure when or why, but at some point sweet things began to disgust you. It was probably the *yerba mate* that enamored you with bitter flavors. Whatever. Not the point. I merely project the images I find deep behind your eyes, and of this particular wharf, strangely, most of what you remember is cement.

You thought it was weird that it wasn't built out of wood and nobody wore white-and-blue striped T-shirts, sailor hats, or whatever else you'd seen in movies: the soggy cotton hats, the beards, the wooden legs – think Popeye and Smee from Disney's *Peter Pan,* though neither of them had beards. Your grandmother bought you *carimañolas* for breakfast and sat you down by a wall overlooking the boats.

You ate in silence.

The wharf was more silent than you imagined. There was no shouting. No hawking of wares or drunk people getting into fights. The air was tepid wind and sputtering engines and river wavelets striking the cement; the waters feeding the mossy overgrowth scattered on the ramp like green veins branching about each other down into the depths, morphing into algae.

The *carimañolas* were nice and warm, freshly made, and tasted better than those you've had before.

"These are made on the day," your grandma said. "They have real *yuca* mashed by hand and fried this morning with actual chunks of beef. They're not like the frozen ones you buy in the city. Doña Norma makes them well. I'd know. I showed her years ago at a church event. And now she has a business of her own."

The *carimañolas* were delicious, claiming the entirety of your attention until a loud horn blasted over the harbor. It was time to go. The boat was leaving. You thought it'd be a good thing you had your tickets, and that you arrived early, because the pier was lined with people trying to squeeze themselves at the last minute, paying double or triple the price, which made them more appetizing for the boat skippers, so most of them boarded even before those who did buy tickets, but you managed to jump in at the very last on the edge of the boat.

You wondered once why if your grandmother knew this happened every single time then why did she bother to arrive early and buy the tickets when she may end up not boarding anyway?

You child! You boy!

You still looked at it from a place of privilege, albeit not unwittingly since you were willing to sympathize, even if you couldn't entirely relate, and so you couldn't understand a simple fact: she couldn't afford to bid for a place on the boat because only the highest price won the bid. All she could do was rely on the system, the process put forth on paper: arrive early, buy a ticket, board the boat. And like this many like her follow the protocols set out by their bureaucracy, helplessly dependent on a structure that is greedy by inclination, by habit, and more often than not by default: because they have no choice, until they claim one, fight for one, and seize it for themselves.

This is why everyone tries to one-up each other. To drive on the side of the road, to live within loopholes and *coimas* and *palancas* - bribes and partisan benefits, because of who you know - because the system will *not* take care of them. Because it wasn't built for their benefit in the first place. And so they have to take care of themselves by swindling and opportunism or, as Panamanians glorified it: *juega vivo.*

She told you this much after you boarded. She was angry. Her face twisted with indignation. Not because it hadn't happened to her before, but because it was now happening to *you* and she felt guilty she had brought her little boy down to her world to see injustice.

Is this all I can give him, she wondered... *he's not used to this kind of discomfort*, she thought, and then you screamed and laughed excitedly at a jumping fish.

She smiled.

She hugged you.

And you hugged her back but kept pointing at the fish as a man sat next to you and told you it was a river trout, that it was gray and shiny to the point of being silver and it tasted nice when made into *ceviche.* He said he'd give you some from his shop when you arrived in Pasiga.

He doesn't care, your grandmother thought. And you didn't. *He's a kid.*

You were ecstatic to be on a boat with your grandma. That is all you knew, all you saw, all there was.

It was all you needed.

***

This following portion lives vividly in your mind. The amount of detail is commendable, though not achieved by any particular effort on your part but by your occasionally, and involuntary, photographic memory.

Whenever I look into our memories from your perspective I see the pictures clearly: you remember the trip under a starlit night, a flash of colors bordering a canyon, the Milky Way a trench across the sky, clouds floating in between as the stars incinerated them mid-flight. Gone and dissipated with no chance of rain. The water was calm and shallow. The boat's wake billowed to the shore as its trail grew and disappeared from the water like pressure on sun-tanned skin. It smelled of gasoline, the boat, but you liked it, somehow, to keep your mind grounded: it was breezy and cold.

She wrapped you tightly in a blanket, though you remember hiding under a plank trying not to vomit. That's the second image in your mind: you, huddled up between a bunch of blankets trying to fall asleep, listening to the man taking a shit from the ship's bow and shouting, "Ese e' mi culo! Ese e' mi culo!"

That's my ass!

And you laughed.

The air smelled of gasoline and shit.

The wind sang of rivulets and fish, far off jumping and splashing on the edge of ripples, sand agitating whatever little shrimp lived between the rocks.

And I know there is no way you could recall these sensory details, I only relate them because I've found them in your memory, however the mind remembered, the impressions did linger, and their effect is found in the affinity you've struck with similar vistas in the future.

Out of all of Nature's gifts, the deafening force of a strong breeze pummeling your ears is your favorite one, but the impossible silence as stars shine on flat water is a close second.

And this trip is where you first experienced it.

There was a small island on the edge of the river. It could've been a patch of coastline, but you remember it as an island and you never asked your grandmother for fear of dispelling the charm. You remember an expanse of beach littered with driftwood and the smell of seaweed, however improbable this was, and you running around jumping from log to log struggling to stand as they rolled under your feet.

Your grandmother went off somewhere, and the rest of the people in the boat had suddenly disappeared, and you were alone. Next thing you remember you're in a man's ramshackle hut waiting for water to boil out of a make-shift stove so you can eat some instant noodles out of an earthen bowl. Somehow you remember it being blue, though again: unlikely.

You ate the noodles and the next memory finds you being chased up a hill by a pig toward the house. The story would stay with you forever because, as your grandma tells it, you were scared, but you were laughing.

You were happy.

CHAPTER 30

Do you remember when you killed that guy in China?

You must've told the story to dozens of people when you were back in Panama, particularly girls you dated. It shed a brooding bad-boy light on you. It made you look tormented, and interesting, or so you thought.

It worked, too.

You did get the girls, and they bought your story. You've always had a knack for victimizing yourself.

Hence, the shit show.

It was sometime in January, or perhaps it was already February, but definitely before March. You started your day early making your way to the park. The memory of the streets is fresh. The smell is what lingers most. The scent of fish and chives rising through the vents. In the mornings, of fried bread-sticks and congee. Fresh durian cut by the side of the road. Fresh *baozi* and *shaomai* steamed in bamboo baskets.

Shaomai in particular was a favorite breakfast of yours. Cheap as fuck, too. Your words. Sticky, glutinous rice wrapped within steamed wonton skins gathered at the top. You remember they looked like mini-pomegranates in your hand: the taste amazing even after the tenth one stuffed down your gullet as you walked along the street.

It's easy for me to narrate your memories to you because you've stored them in this format anyway. They're stored in the Third-Person point of view. Your perceptions are assimilated at a distance, as if I were the only one paying attention all this time. Perhaps, I manifest *because* you externalized every experience.

When you think about it, I have an insight into all your

habits, which led to my awareness. Most *daemons* don't have this. Most people don't feed them as you did me by starving yourself of your own life. By wandering about in perpetual estrangement. Still, the memories are there. And they're yours. This dualism we now enjoy can't be all that bad. Even in solitude, you're not alone.

You remember the taste of *boluobao* mixed with all the sugar and the blank stares following you on the street. You could eat breakfast, lunch, and dinner with a handful of yuan and still have some to spare. You learned the numbers, the quantities of things, and though their hand gestures for numbers were different, you'd learn to speak the numbers before memorizing the gestures.

The number seven, for instance, was made by an upside-down 'L'. All ten numbers could be gesticulated with one hand. It was practical. But learning to speak Mandarin was more practical.

You learned.

You'd think they'd get used to you after seeing you every day, but every time they were surprised to see you. At first, you thought it was because they thought you were a different kid every time, but you were later told that for a foreign fifteen-year-old to be gallivanting around small-town China at all hours of the night was, to say the least, terribly ill-advised, which is why whoever was out prowling the night and saw you carelessly eating snacks on the road must've thought it was a trap.

You defied logic.

Such brazen disregard for personal safety *had* to be a ploy. Later on, a friend of yours said this must've been the reason because even the locals didn't mess around back alleys in the middle of the night. Back home you wouldn't do it, so why you did it there was beyond me, until I realized you did it because you felt you were traveling, exploring, and to you it was no different from walking around in the park. For those lurking behind the proverbial shadows, you were too good to be true, too easy for comfort. And far from being courage it was sheer idiocy, milking the good fortune of the innocent, to whom nothing ever happens.

That night you had dinner from a street cart by the supermarket: some boiled sweet potatoes and steamed parsnip pancakes with some sort of thick sauce and green onions. The latter was more of a breakfast staple, but the vendor still had some. Cold. Chewy. And cheap. You had been looking for some audio cables, RGA red-and-yellow ones, to use on some chest-high speakers you had found at the apartment. You ended up making a make-shift cable from loose copper wires left from an old radio.

The point wasn't the cable but that you had a project, something for which to hunt and occupy yourself. And this is how you spent most of the time, to appease the mental lethargy you constantly found yourself in, going from project to project, finding this cable or that one, this cellphone or the other, a videogame, the smell of a particular type of street food which you couldn't find after tasting everything hawked by the side of the road which, again, should've made you sick but never did.

You must've been such an anomaly for the locals. I mean you were. And you knew. The way they stared in half-amazement and half-disdain: a mix of "how dare you" with – and this happened often - "holy-shit-it-could-be-a-movie-star-so-take-a-picture-just-in-case."

Years later, in Shanghai, you met with other foreigners living in China and learned the staring was a regular occurrence, even in cosmopolitan cities like Shanghai, with building-sized pictures of models and movie stars put there to be stared at, where you mustered almost as many stares as in Huadu.

The shit you pulled in Shanghai is a matter for another time, though, and the astounding luck that kept you safe for those five months defies all bullshit claims you have to be an atheist.

There doesn't have to be a god to be spiritual. My very presence blasts away all your claims to secularism. I'm telling you, the number of times you could've ended up in deep shit but didn't is immeasurable. And we're almost at the alley. It's coming. But we must discuss the mental state you were in before you got there, because it gathered in your mind the right ingredients for the preposterous behavior you put out once you did get there.

Somewhere between the thousandth and millionth time you listened to *Kryptonite* by 3 Doors Down, imagining all sorts of grandiose scenarios like saving the world from aliens to fighting your future self (or extradimensional self) coming to your world to conquer it because his was destroyed, you took your earphones off to listen to a group of kids speaking English to each other. They were Chinese. They knew some English words from movies or from stuffing their face at MacDonald's around the corner – who knows! – and were spouting them at each other in mockery of you being in their vicinity. You found this funny. You weren't the slightest bit offended, and even mustered a look and sent it their way. They stared back. All four of them. And never stopped staring. Even after you'd walked away. You could feel their following gaze.

You were scared.

You put in your earphones to play *Kryptonite* again.

They followed you into the alley. You knew. Half of them were behind you and the other half went around the block to get you from the front. There was a bit of sun left but it's not like it ever made it past the dome of smog, and it was almost nighttime. The alley was dark enough. Dark enough for none to see, but lit enough for you to see each other, to fuck each other up.

There were more of them. They must've thought they could easily beat you up.

But you were an emotionally repressed fuck. And you had a steel bar you found by a dumpster that by the end of the next three minutes was sleek with blood and slipping off your hands.

You always imagined you'd wield it like a sword, one-handed, but you ended up using it as a bat, which annoyed you inordinately because it marked you as thuggish inside your head, a baseball player at best, but not a swordsman, which is what you'd constantly romanticized.

One of them was still conscious against the wall. Heaving. Coughing up blood. Most likely concussed. And you figured it was great because now you got to wield the steel rod as a sword. You wiped it with your hoodie and plunged straight into his left eye, which was ironic because after all the fuzz about swords you ended up using it like a spear. And it was hollow, too, the steel bar – it was more of a pipe, really - so the kid's eyeball was sucked right in. It came right out after you did use the tube like a sword to try and cut his head off, and then you walked away.

You wrapped your hoodie around the tube and brought it with you to the apartment, took your earphones off, and went to take a shower because you were all riled up despite it having all happened in your imagination.

Although nothing happened, you believed if you didn't throw away the hoodie someone would sneak up on your baby sister and beat her up in an alley.

This was the first instance, Orlando, though you didn't know it then, that you experienced your mind's ability to tell itself stories, to take them as truths, and incept itself with lessons learned, failures suffered, and potentials mourned.

As the shower warmed up, steamed up, and the toilet bowl was agitated by the drops like a pothole in the rain, you took one step forward with your right foot, then left, put your right foot back, left foot back, right foot forward, left food forward, right foot back, and said to yourself, "One, two, three, and, then, three…" then jumped back-first into the shower.

This was the first manifestation of what would grow out inside your mind for years to come, what would, clinically, eventually give birth to me:

Obsessive-Compulsive Disorder.

OCD.

CHAPTER 31

So, that's how your grandfather and I met, and I never told you about where we went or what we did, *lijo*, because that's mine to keep.

Those memories are mine to cherish, even now when I know what I know and where I, him, and us, would end up: I still treasure them.

I was happy in them, even as I allowed myself to be saddened by the memory of them. At first I thought they were fake, especially in comparison with the reality in which I later found myself, but then I thought it could be the death of their potential, and that I was sad because I knew their like would never happen again. And I grieved. I grieved because they were now pearls I had to hold on to, golden eggs from a dead hen rotting right before my eyes...

I think of them as keepsakes now, sweet ripe fruit that was delicious then but as time passed it rotted and I was too dumb, too young, too filled with hope and passion that I thought ripe fruit could sway the test of time, that it wouldn't rot, that nostalgia would keep it fresh in its refrigerated cage... but no, *lijo*, ripe fruit goes bad eventually, so you must eat it while it's there, and in the end all you can keep are the seeds: you can make a necklace out of them, put them on the mantelpiece, or on the wall, or do as I did and plant them in the ground, care for them, and see how they grow into sons and daughters and grandchildren, great-grandchildren, and see how the forest grows lush and doesn't care if it was watered with tears instead of rain.

You see, *lijo*, the trees are full of ripe fruit now, all from that one seed which had its use and I buried in the ground. It would be foolish to hate the tree for ceasing to be the fruit it once was, so I don't hate your grandfather. God forgives and so do I. Not because it's deserved but because it frees me of the hate, rids me of the rot, and all is well. Because I'm okay. Because I chose to be okay. And that's enough.

This is the generation God chose to throw me into, and him, which resulted in you being thrown into the one where you are now.

I've prayed for clarity many times, *lijo*, to see at least a glimpse of the point of it all, because there *must* be a point, because I want there to be, and I believe God does listen to what we want.

It's fine about your grandfather. It's fine if all the good in him lies in the future, in all the good things that will exist because *he* existed, because *I* chose to forgive and plant the seed instead of crushing it underfoot. That is also fine, *lijo*, even if you make the same mistakes he did, because we're not perfect, not all fruit ripens and some is eaten by worms or birds or lingers in the ground to compost... but it's fine, like I said. But enough about fruit.

I went back to the city after the summer break. The Willoughby's had taken a trip to New York. They had fun but were happy to be back, happy to see me. They brought me gifts and T-shirts from the Big Apple. As the days went on I noticed they were a little different, a longing look in their eyes. Will would zone out and *Señora* would stare out in a daze and even do the dishes herself sometimes. The children, too, looked bored after a while, unstimulated, and soon enough they sat me down to tell me they were thinking about moving out of Panama, that they will, in fact, and they wanted me to come with them.

They said they'd pay for my education, that I'd have a good life there, a degree, and that I was a part of the family and they would love to see me grow and be a professional in the United States. But it was the same story, *lijo*, as old as time, and what better way to describe than with a cliché, because it is a cliché, as

old as time as well: I was pregnant.
    I stayed.

***

Your grandfather and I got married and got a house in La Mesa, eventually some land in Pasiga… you remember Pasiga, right?

CHAPTER 32

Of course you remember.

We were reviewing that the other day. The mother pig chasing you? Yea, that was fun to watch you experience, even in my dormant stage. But those memories are best left untouched, you see, they're so distant and embellished in nostalgic fancy that it would do you harm to smear them with the truth. So, how about that? Let shit be.

You had a nightmare last night. Sleeping with your headphones on to cancel out the noise gives you lucid dreams. At first, you could say anything in them. You struggled to bring out a word, and if you did it came out broad, as if in slow motion, but now you can speak a little better, though you mostly scream. Still, it's good for your brain. Gives it strength, though you've always feared your mind as if a monster lived in there. That's why you've never done any drugs and you've become leery of alcohol with the years. Assuming *I'm* the demon, you fear I won't you give back, and you'll be stuck behind your eyes watching me go about my days. 'Your' days.

You dumb fuck. Do you think I want the burden of existing? Do you think I'm thirsting to go out into the world and walk around and do *what*, exactly? I'm afraid, too. I'm afraid of living a life where *you're* the one inside *my* head, watching what I do, and fucking it up in there.

Do you think *you're* the sane one? Without me, you'd make even less sense to yourself. I'm not saying you might as well go and shoot up heroine, but don't say it's because of me.

You are terrified of having to play *my* role because you know you'd fuck it up.

CHAPTER 33

A typical morning began with tense deliberations about which foot to get off the bed.

Well, no.

That's not right.

You slept on your back, and so you first had to decide whether to roll over to your right or to your left to get off the bed. This took a bit because it was tough to decide between your sister being run over and her being kidnapped in a van.

You lay there in bed ruminating whether she'd be worse off having survived or dying from either and, naturally, the entire burden of those futures clung to your decision of either rolling over to the right or to the left. Choices. Choices, indeed, were the paralyzing factor.

I'm not sure if you thought it was Free Will, or perhaps delusions of grandeur what made you think these dimensional crossroads relied on your choices. Perhaps it was your narcissism beginning to show itself, perhaps it was the OCD, for real – I know it was not *not* the OCD, at least – or maybe: maybe it was the overwhelming feeling of helplessness, of loneliness.

And yet...

It wasn't so bad. And I know there is no metric for emotional pain, that is exemplifies relativity, metaphorically speaking. A prick can be as painful as being impaled depending on your state of mind – of your emotional stamina at the time. And I know comparisons are pointless: just because another broke two arms doesn't mean your single broken arm doesn't hurt.

Anyway...

Once you got the getting-up part done, it was time to

choose which way you turned to get off the bed, then which foot touched the ground first, whether you stood up or did a little skip... I could go on, as it did go on, like this, though I'm not sure it's fair to blame it entirely on me. I mean, I did come from *it*, but I wasn't *It*, either.

Shit got real when you had to get dressed. Picking underwear was a shit show. Socks. A shirt. Everything had an outcome, every choice weighed on you as if the world would change because of it, and while there are theories suggesting this to be true, the part where every outcome is a terrible one is entirely in your head.

Scientifically, what you're bastardizing is called the Many-Worlds Interpretation (MWI), notoriously exemplified by Schrodinger's quantum-mechanical thought-experiment of the cat-in-the-box: most famously called "Schrodinger's cat."

Everyone is familiar with the paradox: the cat is *both* alive and dead as long as the box remains closed. So long as we do not perceive the 'reality' of whether the cat is dead or alive, we remain at a dimensional crossroads.

According to the theory, every choice, no matter how minute, creates a 'fork' in the timeline. Two roads diverge, creating two different worlds, let's say: one in which the cat is alive, and one in which the cat is dead. The fork is exemplified by the unopened box.

You are so terrified of choosing the wrong world that you stare at the box and do nothing. You glorify possibility at reality's expense, and the problem with this is that possibility is infinite: a skilled imagination will even make it palpable – but it's ultimately unreal.

You freeze at the opportunity of choice, valuing the many options, the many choices with their many worlds, over the single one you can live.

You're afraid, and so you wait for the choice to be made for you.

In Schrodinger's experiment, you'd take no action. You would stare at the box until you felt the smell of a corpse. You'd stand in time as if in a conveyor belt, riding wherever the forces led - and there! You now live in the world where the cat is dead.

But see, you didn't choose. You were paralyzed with indecision and all this does is breed dishonesty within yourself. And what is worse, you plunge into a vortex of hindsight, evaluating all that you may have missed had you opened the box, had you flipped it over, had you shaken it. Had you fucking taken action!

But what is the point then?

When it came to it, you cowered. You froze, and there's no point in trying to think of it in hindsight.

From a quantum perspective, Hindsight is absurd.

Hindsight takes the outcome of one timeline of events and smears it over an entirely different universe.

It is sheer, ignorant consequentialism.

The outcome in contention exists only because of the collective choices made before it. In a universe where those choices have been different, the situation leading to that outcome may not exist at all, and asserting that it would is no more than hopeful, uninformed hubris.

Say you went out in white jeans. You go on for lunch and spill soy sauce on them.

You say to yourself, "And I almost wore black jeans today! Had I worn those the sauce would be unnoticeable."

Wrong.

What you're doing is you're taking the outcome of one universe – the one in which you spilled soy sauce on yourself – and transposing it into a hypothetical universe in which you wore black jeans.

The layers of assumptions are exponential.

You assume that in that universe you didn't die right after putting on the black jeans, that you then continued to not die throughout the day until lunchtime, that the sushi restaurant was open on that day and not closed because a car had crashed right into it or there was a gas leak or the owner didn't feel like working. You assumed you weren't held up in traffic and had to go eat somewhere else… possibilities *ad nauseam.*

This way of thinking, common to us all, is described in the Uniformity Principle, as coined by David Hume in his book *An Inquiry Concerning Human Understanding.* In David Hume's words, it is custom what "makes us expect for the future, a similar train of events with those which have appeared in the past."

The Uniformity Principle assumes that future situations, in all probable worlds of the Many-Worlds Interpretation, must be similar to a preceding situation in our current pocket of existence.

The future resembles the past.

If Y has once followed X, then Y *must* follow in a world where X exists.

Hindsight is born, dressed in assumptions so bright and galactic that while it may resemble truth, it isn't.

My point, Orlando, is don't waste your time with hindsight and keep moving.

The best way to change reality is to take action now. The surest way to redirect a vector is to modify the force *you* exert on it. Open the box slowly if you would, or walk away and not give a shit.

But if you would give a shit, here's the formula… if it helps:

$$i\hbar\frac{\partial}{\partial t}\Psi(\mathbf{r},t) = \hat{H}\Psi(\mathbf{r},t)$$

Existential homilies and quantum treatises aside – though I hope to pin some science to what goes on inside your head… for contrast – you actively perceived the so-called dimensional crossroads with every choice you made. And yes, our choices do matter. The butterfly in Brazil may set off a tornado in Texas - Chaos Theory and The Butterfly Effect and all that – and there *is* a level of control to be taken from the ownership of one's small choices, and the actions related to those choices, and all the cosmic reverberations ensuing from whether you fart into the couch cushion or lift your ass a little bit. But when you can barely handle the intricacies of the next minute, Orlando, it's not just delusional but plain arrogant to presume you can measure every ripple your every action makes.

It is not your burden because it can't be. It can't be because it shouldn't be. The universe *must* have a better option than *you* to fathom its micro and macro causalities, and that you would even consider yourself remotely competent for this is pure narcissism - one of your key flaws to which we'll get to later - but the point is: everything matters so much, in such a grand scale, that in your spectrum of existence, as you are, nothing does!

You did get it eventually, or stopped giving a fuck, which is how you've dealt with healing and most of your experiences, but if merely not giving a fuck about OCD helped those with a more drastic version of the illness, they would also take it. They wouldn't ask questions of why it went away. They'd let it be, as you did, even one as mild as yours is, and allow it to turn into the fun, witty *daemon* you now love so much.

A smarter person would realize it was writing and journaling that helped you.

Artists love that shit. Calling it a muse, or a guardian angel, the ego – whatever. They love romanticizing the shit show in their heads. It breeds devotion, a measure of indulgence, martyrdom, a bit of peace, even, to bring the world art at their own expense.

So, call me what you will, but go with it.

Go make something!

CHAPTER 34

I don't think you understand the historical relevance of your father's little smuggling stint.

Perhaps he doesn't know it either, and it was no more than a side-hustle to him - who knows? - I mean, I'm sure *he* does... you should ask. But this is what I gathered.

Much attention has been given to the impact of blue jeans in Eastern Europe during the Cold War. The iconic picture of jean-wearing youths sitting on the Berlin Wall is a prime example. Levi Strauss & Co was a key player in what gradually became a cultural movement in the Eastern Bloc pervaded by Western Culture and, particularly, Americana.

Jeans became a symbol of opposition to the Communist Regime, surreptitiously transacted among the youth of East of the Berlin Wall, Russia, and all over Eastern Europe.

It became a commodity, beyond being a symbol of status (due to its exorbitant price averaging half a month's pay), and on to become an emblem of freedom. Soon enough, anyone caught hawking or as little as wearing jeans began to disappear.

To the Communist Regime, blue jeans represented capitalist oppression, Western propaganda, and an insult to their interpretation of the Marxist democratic ideal. Their mistake, as it often happens, was that by disavowing something they created a symbol for their own opposition. By condemning jeans, they gave the people a sigil by which to rally.

With jeans came a new wave of Americana seeping into popular youth culture in Communist countries: Rock n' Roll, motorcycles, Hollywood, dancing. Everything American was game to be used as an emblem for freedom, not necessarily because the United States was the only free country in the world, but because by using American culture as a chant for opposing oppression it became, by juxtaposition, a symbol of freedom.

The government began to give way soon enough, allowing for the limited sale of jeans, even going as far as making off-brand versions of it, thinking the charm was merely the clothing itself. For a percentage of the jean-wearing population it was, indeed, mere fashion, to be 'cool,' and so by this means they managed to separate the revolutionaries from the posers, though inadvertently they also made it possible for more people to wear jean-looking trousers which, to the untrained eye, looked like the Movement against the Communist Regime had grown in supporters.

This concession by the Communist Regime suggested they wanted to avoid a war, and to the revolutionaries, this marked a pivotal moment in their opposition, because the best time to fight tyranny is when it doesn't want a war.

It doesn't want it because it has something to lose, and that's the very people who oppose it: their allegiance, their submission and acquiescence - their doing nothing.

Words have power.

The advent of Communism, Nazism, and any radical ideology, including Democracy in its time, began with words. When tyranny first takes over, and is afraid of being overthrown, they ensure to deprive their people of words as much as relieving them of weapons. A tyrant will chop heads in hopes of killing the idea, thinking this is where it lives, but an idea lives on words: words to spread it, to explain it, to amplify it with metaphors and poetry, to incite it and adapt it to any obstacles that may manifest. In trying to extinguish it, Tyranny spreads the idea and rekindles it by using the wrong agent to put it out, like water on an electrical fire.

The intricacies and nuances of this have been elucidated in numerous articles and books written on the subject. And this isn't a political manifesto. This is about you, your past, your multi-dimensional present, and your probable, one would hope, flourishing future.

I tell you this to give a background to your father's story, and to strike the point that oppression starts by having evil things happen and there being no consequence to them.

And self-oppression is no different.

He would bring the jeans from Mexico into Cuba, not from the United States, and so the transaction wasn't as symbolically egregious as smuggling them from the United States which, due to the embargo with Cuba, would've been a more serious tier of trafficking than from Mexico. Nonetheless, the message remained: blue jeans represented capitalism, and that was enough of a 'Fuck you' to the Cuban Communist Regime.

Your father still laughs at how the Cubans didn't speak a word of English. They called blue-jeans *bluyines* (pronounced bloo-jeen-ehs in Spanish) regardless of their color. There were *bluyines blancos, bluyines negros,* and, most amusingly redundant to him, *bluyines azules.*

Jeans weren't the only commodity he brought, but from music to electronics, to snacks and American candy, by far the most curious item was *Kotex* Maxi-pads. He'd wear the jeans in customs, layers over layers, which limited the range of sizes he could bring. Curvy Cubans were out of luck, and whichever woman got her hands on a pair of jeans would make a double statement by wearing men's clothes on top of them being banned.

A shipment of *Kotex* was trickier because if he got caught he could hardly explain why he needed them on his person, on account of his not having a uterus and, upon a cursory inspection of his anatomy, the discovery of a non-ovulating penis.

The barter system was simple. He had goods the people wanted, and they were willing to trade anything for them because they had little of everything, and of what little they did have or were allowed to have, they paid handsomely. Your father was in it for the fun of it, and of fun the Cubans had plenty.

Men showed him around the island to all the cool places

and nice restaurants, while the women favored him for being 'un hombre de negocios,' a businessman. Still, most people referred to him as 'el buhonero pana,' which loosely translates to The Panamanian Peddler, though the goods he 'peddled' were the opposite of cheap or trinkets, but it made the local authorities shrug him off as small-time. And he was. It's not like he had a cartel going on, but the Communist Regime, as he described it, is often overzealous, and so a little taint on their so-called utopia is an insult to its ideals, a bit of white cutting through all the red looks too much like the American flag and, "eso no se puede, chico."

Can't have any of that.

The one day he almost got caught made the fun all too real for him. He walked through the metal detector bedecked in layers of denim stuffed with maxi-pads, and one of the younger cops thought he was the first to notice the rarity of the tourist's clothing in such a hot climate.

The other cops were used to looking the other way, but that was as much as they'd be willing to do, and even that was risky enough. In short, they would not stop the eager cop if he caught your father smuggling. They would not stop him from taking your father to the *campo de fusilamiento,* where criminals were shot against a wall and then thrown into a ditch. They would, however, 'confiscate' the *bluyines* before shooting him to avoid poking any holes in them, and it was here your father realized he was worth less than the thick layer of denim he was currently drenching with cold sweat.

After all the applause and flirtation and false appreciation, he'd be shot naked and buried with a bunch of maxi-pads sucking in the wrong kind of blood.

Jeans, you see, *denim*, was an idea: whether it was freedom, or luxury, opposition or vanity, or how well they contoured a Cuban ass mid-twirl, all those things were worth more to them than your father's replaceable life.

El buhonero pana was never seen again.

Some say he was never real. And your father became another salty sailor looking for fun, bringing his money into Cuba and not the other way around.

A man doing his sea-time, yearning to go back home.

CHAPTER 35

The chicken feet were running out.

Your mother had written tomes of recipes by the time the last bag ran out. *A la criolla, al ajillo, en su jugo, asadas, hervidas, en salsa blanca, roja, fritas.* And so on.

Mayrita grew fond of them. It helped her with her teething, and it made her feel grown to see herself eating the same food as the adults.

There was talk of the invasion being over soon. Disappearances were becoming less and less frequent. The looting was coming down, albeit because there wasn't anything left to loot. Politicians turned vocal, public. Word was the Americans had caught *El Cara De Piña.* And they wanted to avoid a war.

Panamanians, like the jean-wearing East-Berliners, well understood this was the right time to fight against tyranny – when it didn't want a war – but this was a different type of fight. This was a concession, deemed wise by many when compared to the alternative. It wasn't a battle against tyranny, per se. It was choosing the lesser evil. The least violence.

Guillermo Endara, on the 20th of December, 1989, accepted the democratic presidency of Panama from the United States in Fort Clayton. In his words, as reported by *The Independent*, "morally, patriotically, civically I had no other choice". No *better* choice.

This was a favoring of the wolf over the hyena, which was fine because the hyena is known to kill for sport and laugh about it. The wolf only kills for profit, which cuts into a country's skin less often and in different places, granting it more time to heal old wounds.

To recover.

Your mother was chopping *aji chombo* to throw into the last batch of chicken feet, because for all the history playing itself out beyond her window, and for all the politics argued, and however blatantly democracy was being reduced to a technicality, your mother understood there can hardly be anything more important than a toddler asking for a snack. To her, a politician's most incendiary opinion is no more important than that of a child's most fleeting of fancies. And with this, no sensible parent would disagree.

Your mother wasn't Mayrita's mother. And though she would never see Mayrita again after her real mother was finally able to pick her up, it was Mayrita who taught her how to be a mother. Mayrita taught your mother the kind of parenting she used on you: may the world blaze beyond that window, you shall be safe and fed within her walls.

Nobody knows or dared ask where Mayrita's mother had been during the invasion, but it sufficed to say that she came as soon as it was humanly possible for her, with much room still left in her heart for Mayrita to carry on breaking, as only daughters can, when the little girl asked your mother who this woman was and what she wanted with her chicken feet.

It hurt, for a bit, before both women smiled.

As painful as it was for Mayrita's mother, this type of animosity could only be directed at a familiar face. Toddlers are often shy instead of rude to strangers. This rudeness meant Mayrita recognized her mother, even if subconsciously, and after so long away, living through whatever it was she lived through, her daughter's recognition was enough for this woman to be happy again.

Your mother was twenty-two years old then, a little under two years before you were born, starting the new decade, in 1990, to live out her last year of not being a mother. She was almost twenty-four when she had you. Twenty-three, she was, when she decided she'd keep you.

Abortion was, still is, illegal in Panama, and worse yet, almost unanimously opposed. And whether it was civil law or religious duty what made your mother decide to keep you despite what in moments of anger she has suggested your father's preference had been, whether it was the need to replace Mayrita or that inherent cry for life to perpetuate itself - whatever her reasons - may we even call it love, she *would* have her baby.

She *would* be a mother. And would have snacks for her boy every morning, cook a whole damn meal at 5 am for him to bring back untouched in the afternoon, drive hours each day to take him and pick him up from school because he *had* to go to the best one they could afford.

And yes, she would lose her shit over stupid shit and be tough when you'd need her to be tender. She'd fuck up, many times, because – you mindless fuck! – she wasn't much older than you were when you were getting drunk at nightclubs.

She did all this without your education, without your travels and experience, without much self-scrutiny or discernment that what had been inculcated in her by churches and convention and – guess what? – despite all the shit she said and the fucked up things she did… whatever you may hold against her… she had the fortitude to send you away so you may build yourself a mind of your own, even as she suffered how you looked down on her when you came back.

She didn't know there's a whole world outside of Panama who doesn't give a shit about anyone's opinion, and so she shouldn't care about what other people think… but she did care, and she wanted *you* to care because she thought it'd make things easier for you, which it was worse, because you were lying to yourself. And to her.

Neither of you is perfect.

You taught her there was more to motherhood than keeping you fed, and she taught you to make shit happen for yourself, that life doesn't tolerate much sulking before it looks the other way.

And hey, it was all the convention and religion and 'backwardness' which made her choose to keep you in the end. And whatever ill this mindset may have caused in other people's lives, it'd grant you yours and at most annoyed you a little bit later on.

So how about you let shit go?

How about you tell her what's in your mind.

"It's okay, mom," you should say, "I know you were young and angry and I get it. I see you with my daughter, and you're an excellent grandmother. The whole point is that she enjoys better things, and why shouldn't this begin with her enjoying a better version of you? I'm so happy she has you. I'm so happy I still have you, as you are now, and I get to see us enjoy better versions of each other. I was as unprepared to be a son as you were to be a mother, and that's okay. We made it."

CHAPTER 36

She pulled the *pesada de nance* out of the fridge.

"I made it last night," your grandmother said, "but I don't have any cheese."

"I don't like cheese in it anyway," you said. "Thank you!"

"You're just saying that…"

"I mean it."

"I suppose I don't like it much with cheese either, *lijo*."

"I can go buy some if you want."

"That's ok. It's not necessary, *lijo*."

"It's cheap."

"That doesn't make it necessary," she said. "When you do away with certain pleasures for a while, *lijo*, you come to naturally not crave them anymore. I like my *pesada* without cheese now, and I don't want to change that. You won't be here all the time, and cheese isn't cheap for me."

She sat down in front of you and asked about her granddaughter, about you shipping out again after barely being home a couple of weeks, and you forgot all about how she lost her temper a little bit.

You told her you'd like to write a book about her stories, thought she didn't like the word 'story' as much she preferred 'experiences' because, as she said, "calling them stories makes it sound like they were fun or left entirely in the past," and they were neither.

She asked if you'd like to listen to her now, but you said no. You said you'd like to sit and talk and eat your *pesada* with her 'in the moment.'

There's enough time for the past in the future, and you like your present lived.

She smiled.

***

You could never reach your grandmother on her phone, and the signal was bad whenever you did.

She didn't know how to use her smartphone beyond picking up phone calls, and that was still in progress. You asked your cousin to record her and send the videos to you. It was tough because the videos were long, and she didn't have enough storage in her phone to save them at first. Then, she didn't have enough data to send them over to you.

You didn't realize the inconvenience of your request, and she'd never admit it came to her at a cost: deleting songs or other videos she had taken on her phone, buying a phone card from the store to get enough data to send the videos over to you.

The author James Baldwin once wrote, "Anyone who had ever struggled with poverty knows how extremely expensive it is to be poor."

When you noticed they were a lot better off than her neighbors, since many around town would come to her for a meal, your grandmother said, "They don't know how to be poor."

She said she had "the intrepid heart of the humble." When the pandemic struck, she couldn't linger on the couch as some fortunate people did. She got back up and found a way. She made hats, masks, designed patterns. She seized the opportunity.

Hardship isn't new for her.

It's not the first time life delivered her a situation. While you're still learning the basics, Orlando, she's living her thesis.

Help isn't coming. Life owes you nothing. Help yourself.

You must admit you felt detached from her reality, even a bit selfish and ashamed when you thought about your conversations, but she never recriminated. She never held your ignorance of her tribulations against you. She was happy you couldn't relate, that you had no experience of the shortages she had, the dearth, even if to you *she* was happier than you were, and this is why you were always so drawn to her. This is why you admired her: needing so little, lacking so much (in your perspective), and yet giving everything.

The videos arrived after a week, and you didn't realize until then that you wanted them recorded not because it would be easier to play them back, but because it would've been inconvenient to sit down and listen to her. Because you're a terrible listener and you may have forgotten all you heard.

You didn't realize, then, that she'd much rather be listened to and forgotten, than remembered but ignored.

***

"*Hola, lijo,*" she began, "I'll continue where we left off, yes?"

"Please."

The *pesada* on her hand looked delicious. The phone shook in your cousin's hands as your grandmother spoke.

She hadn't heard your grandma's story.

***

I won't tell you the details of how or when it happened, *lijo*, though you know the why – yes, it was as simple a reason as being friendly, charming – you see, when your standards have been lowered as far down as mine had, for men, even the slightest gesture of attention feels grand, focused, and oh so flattering, as sad as it may sound.

And if you're thinking of Mr. Willoughby, I didn't see him as a man. He was my boss, and also a white man, a foreign man, and the plane of his existence was so astronomically separate from mine, the gap so dark a chasm, so abysmally dug out by centuries of culture and societal norms, that he was more an entity than anything else, as real but as impersonal as a monument.

I remember it fondly, though. That summer. With your grandfather. Even if it's all tarnished now, cheapened by the actions he has taken since. I could say it had to happen because it gave me your aunt, and your uncles and your mom, that I endured it because it gave me your cousins, your daughter... you, *lijo*. But I have faith that it all would've happened anyway.

God would've made it so.

You would've all existed as you do know. Maybe not in the same house, and maybe you would've had a different face, but your soul would've existed, as inexorably enmeshed with mine as it is now. But that is all I'll say about that summer because what mattered of it came later.

I went back to work shortly before the summer ended. The kids had to go shopping for school supplies, and Mr. Willoughby was back at work and so was *Señora.* I remember she was very proud of having a job, said it was *progressive* – and she assumed I didn't know what the word meant so she explained it to me, not knowing the Bible is teeming with words much bigger than hers – but I didn't understand how it was progressive, *lijo,* because where I come from nobody can afford not to work, man or woman, and the fact that you can support a whole family with one working member, man or woman, is in my mind the 'progressive' thing.

But I did learn a lot by working for them, *lijo,* though not necessarily in the academic sense, even if I did learn some history and math through helping the children with their homework. I learned because I had free time, a luxury I never had before.

They gave me a private space, which I used to read and keep a journal. Back in the country, I constantly hustled for money. I worried about what would happen at home with all the work I was made to do. I was always a shout away. My stepmother, my uncle, my aunt, with all their unfounded animosity made worse when paired with my father's indifference: How much of an insult it must've been for him, to have been burdened with two daughters who, to his dismay, he couldn't even sell and was left without a profit. At a loss, even, because "we've been feeding you so far."

But the Willoughby's gave me a room for myself. They called it *El cuarto de empleada,* which loosely translates to The

Maid's Quarters, but in Spanish it's a bit more reductive. There's a measure of class distinction to it. *El Cuarto De Empleada* is more like The Servant's Closet: a door you can knock on at any hour and expect a grateful smile, outside of which you don't have to be careful of waking someone up if you happen to come back drunk in the middle of the night, inside of which dwells a loyal creature, of clever yet submissive disposition, of a calm demeanor, obedient but at the same time graceful enough to make it look voluntary.

It was certainly a nuanced relationship, *lijo*, because while they wanted a servant, they didn't want it said of them they were the kind of people who had, or worse yet, *needed* one.

Still, I was grateful, and by choice willing, because they had given me this space of my own. Even if it was at times invaded, it was safe, and that was more than I had experienced before they came into my life. A friend of mine called it *A Room of One's Own*. She said it was a book by Virginia Woolf.

My friend liked to read, like you, *lijo*, and so she would often reference some book to validate her sympathy. It gave her the notion that she understood.

She didn't.

But it did give her the disposition to listen, which I liked.

And I certainly like it in you, *lijo,* because believe me I would never wish for you to understand. I pray to God that when you listen to misfortune the most you can do is empathize. There is no wisdom in pain for mere sake of it. Life will find its way to teach you its lessons, and it'll be more in tune with the path you're taking.

God spares no one, but he saves everyone, loves everyone, and denies no soul the chance to rise above. Hardship will come, so do not feel left out, *lijo*, I can see it in your eyes sometimes. Enjoy the privilege. I'm glad you have it.

The lessons learned from poverty do not outweigh the suffering. And no measure of guilt will do anything to help those in need. If you would help, *lijo:* listen, learn, and use your good fortune to mend another's lack of it.

That's all, and more than most people do anyway.

One day, *Señora* was on the phone talking to a friend.
I was doing the dishes.
She was going on about how it's so good of her that she's employing a 'local,' and how nice it felt to see me grow more confident, whatever that meant. She told her friend about when they showed me the ocean, and how grateful I was, how good it felt to bring wonder to my eyes, though I mostly remember being called a bastard and a whore, however beautiful the scenery was at the time, but that's on me to have chosen that memory to overpower the other.

I was doing the dishes, not an arm's length away from her, and it amazed me how she could talk about me as if I weren't standing right next to her, as if I only existed when she chose to summon me to her world by perceiving me into it.

My friend called it quantum-something. She said it was like existing in a cloud of probability, or possibility – she couldn't remember the word exactly – and I could only materialize from that cloud into an instance of myself whenever I was perceived, acknowledged, by *her*.

She said we could all do this. Me, too, even, whenever I felt like being alone in a crowded place.

I thought if this was true and the world exists only by God's perception, all He needs to do for all to be destroyed is *blink.* I thought it all very interesting, though unnecessarily complicated. And *Señora* was rude, plain and simple, but I didn't mind, because at the end of the day I went into my room and read my Bible and thought about your grandfather, or at least who I thought he was, and whether or not he'd be happy to know I was pregnant.

CHAPTER 37

You had a couple of days left of quarantine, and it was all coming to a close.

You'd get to, *have* to, leave the small room you were in.

You thought about a painting you saw online: *The Garden of Earthly Delights,* by Hieronymus Bosch. And you wondered what it would be like if you modeled your life after it. You'd have to make it like a *triptych*: a work in three sections, painted or carved, hinged in between so it can either be shown open or shut.

You thought you could make a metaphor of it, but then you shrugged it off as yet more preposterous fancy. You considered the back panels, which become the front when the triptych is closed, and of what you would paint of it. A beginning, perhaps, as Bosch did? Or maybe some representation of causality, an allusion, if you will – might I be so presumptuous! – to *me*?

But the notion was born and remains a notion, which is the problem with most of your artistic thought. Even if an idea were to be born and die as fast as it arose, there would at least be a beginning with an ending. A thing, in itself, to its entirety. But you walk around full of notions, ideas, and possibility; and while at first this may be artistic, or at least worthy of inspiration, it becomes untenable to the brain, and it perturbs whatever monsters might dwell within you.

It perturbs *me,* and we come back to quantum metaphors, Orlando, because I fucking love them. There's so much we don't know about quantum physics that most of it still borders along the brightly-colored coasts of art, and so I find it relatable and a reliable source of allusions.

Just look at the alliterative candy I just wrote!

See, you carry yourself in a perpetual state of superposition, your mind a vast cloud of possibility. Ideas, notions, fanciful prospects, and fits of originality, all float about your mind unrealized, ready to materialize as 'things' whenever you perceive them by granting them your attention, a pocket of air in this doomed soliloquy you call life, and it is this, my friend, what has become to us, to *me*, to *you*, and to everyone in your life who has put up with it till now, unsustainable.

I think you think - which in truth is a euphemism for 'I know you think,' – because *believe me*, I know – that to ponder possibilities is as good as realizing them. And by realizing, I mean making them *real*, into solid particles rejoicing under disciplined attention, perceived into steady fruition, and if you continue to treat your opportunities as you do, it is no different than plunging their heads into the water only to wrench them from the brink of drowning.

It is as complicated, and as preposterous, as that last sentence is structured, and its circuitous subject should by no means be mistaken for depth of thought.

All complexity is shallow.

The truth is deep but simple.

Who knows? It may even be 42.

You expect too much of yourself, of life, and put too much confidence in the probability of you dying within the hour being statistically low, but no rational morsel of your mind could ever say it was impossible, not with a straight face, and so why do you stand on such fickle ground? Habit? Entitlement, I'd say. Perhaps custom – if I'm to give your narcissism some philosophical tinge – in the vein of David Hume, again, to quote:

> "Custom, then, is the great guide of human life. It is that principle alone which renders our experience useful to us, and makes us expect, for the future, a similar train of events with those which have appeared in the past. With-

out the influence of custom, we should be entirely ignorant of every matter of fact beyond what is immediately present to the memory and senses. We should never know how to adjust means to ends, or to employ our natural powers in the production of any effect. There would be an end at once of all action, as well as of the chief part of speculation."

You behave as you do because you've never had to behave otherwise. You privileged, entitled *fuck*! But you should know it's not your fault. You should know it's like your grandma said, "no measure of guilt can cure another's suffering."

It would be an insult to the hard work your parents and your grandparents and all the generations before them put forth so you were born with that very privilege, but as much as it isn't yours to mar with guilt, it isn't yours to squander. And it sure as shit won't be on me to be the reason for pilfering their work. Your work. Your possibility. Our *capacity*.

So go on, now.

Like your daughter says, "Wake up, Daddy," her little hands tapping on your face. "It's sunny out!"

CHAPTER 38

Now, what kind of Latin American writers would we be – since I surely get a claim to your ethnicity – if we don't add some Magical Realism to the mix?

I'd say we're halfway through the shit show, and our readers have all noticed the change in both our voices. Writing does that. Though silent, it shows how your mind speaks.

Everyone in La Mesa knows about your grandmother. She's the kind of woman who exudes tenderness, who could sway the fiercest rage with passive smiles. When you went to church with her, she was, to you, among all the statues of saints and crosses and white doves soaring in the clouds, the single true embodiment of goodness. She is the promise of religion finally fulfilled, though rarely found. And it's nothing so cheap as saying she's 'a saint' or she can do no wrong, but that she's known the good and the ugly, seen them both weld into her scars and mingle on her fists, her eyes, and after all that: she still chose goodness with a smile.

She was making *buñuelos* in the backyard. Your grandfather was cranking the grain mill screwed into an old log, the corn squeezing into a large bowl. You finished the last batch and handed the bowl over to your grandmother. The priest was on his way.

She asked you to hurry.

CHAPTER 39

The priest announced himself with a loud *"Buenos días!"* and walked through the house to meet you in the garden.

He was Colombian. You noticed his *cutarras* right away. Tight, leather sandals dug into his skin. A Panamanian folkloric footwear without much for foot support other than a thin slab of wood or leather. It couldn't have been comfortable to walk in those, you thought, and it certainly couldn't be good for his knees. But you were sure he did it to fit in with the locals.

He was an affable man in his mid-forties or early fifties, and though his name escapes you like that of any person you meet only once, you do remember the conversation. He pulled up an old cinder block and sat in front of you. There was a plastic table in between. Your grandfather offered him a drink. The priest thanked him but declined.

"You must be Rin's grandson," he began, "the one who works at sea, right?"

"Yes," you said. "Nice to meet you."

"Good to meet you, son. Must be nice to be back on land, yes?"

He had already annoyed you. It *was* nice to be on land because you were gone for much longer than you usually were, but he didn't know that. He assumed you must not like being at sea, much like how most people in Panama twist up their faces when you say you live in a place with four seasons.

"Oh, but it gets so cold up there," they'd say, "that's terrible."

As if it were a struggle to wake up to silent, snowy mornings in the woods, to take a walk among the maples and oaks and evergreen trees nestling fluffy squirrels on their branches. Because surely *everyone* in Japan, or Canada, or Norway, or any other place with four seasons lived in perpetual misery, craving the clammy, humid heat of the tropics.

But you also get annoyed at stupid shit. The man only meant you must've missed your grandma, and he was right.

"Yes," you said, "it's been a while since I've had my grandmother's cooking. I missed it."

"Your grandmother is an excellent cook. I've been waiting all week since she invited me over for breakfast last Sunday."

You smiled.

Noticing the accent you asked him if he was Colombian.

"I'm glad this assignment is close to home," he said. "Colombia is a short plane ride away."

You realized now he must've spent a long time away from his loved ones, and so he could relate to you being away. You felt bad for being annoyed.

"Where else have you been assigned?" you asked.

"Mostly in Europe."

"That's nice. Where else?"

"I did do some time in Kenya."

This piqued your interest because of how he said it, "did some time,'" and particularly because he began to hyperventilate right after.

His eyes stared through you into some distant memory, or a much too recent one, judging from the terror in his eyes. Wherever his mind was, he was horrified. He fell. Your grandfather had no idea what to do, and you stared blankly.

Your grandmother heard the noise and rushed out of the house, held the priest's head, and cradled it onto her chest. The priest mumbled things in an unknown language you later learned was Swahili. You recognized some broken English. Some Spanish. Everything puked out a million miles a second as his mind reeled inside his head.

This was the first time you saw it happen.

The moment your grandmother squeezed him against her

chest, her forearms lean with hard-earned muscle, the priest fell into a deep sleep. He let the air out his nose for what felt like minute. He opened his eyes and apologized. Your grandfather helped him up as you helped your grandmother.

She tapped him on his shoulder and got up to fetch the *buñuelos*.

CHAPTER 40

How much out there remains unknown to you?

Your recent interest in space and quantum physics, the dynamics of relativity, whether or not traveling in space can dilate time – it can – has sent your mind into a million flights of fancy. You think of leaving this project behind to work on a sci-fi novel. You consider going back to that fantasy novel you began a bunch of years ago, about the nymphs, and you wonder why is it you've never finished a project.

You can't even call yourself a failure, because you haven't even tried, and can't ask you when it ends because I'm still wondering when it began.

Can you tell me, Orlando, when did it begin?

But maybe this is your process.

Maybe this is how you rid yourself of all the creative dust you've let plaster on your brain. Is this right? Is this what your subconscious is doing? Are you shaking off the barnacles from your mind, ready to set sail? If so, I've got to tell you, creating for creation's sake will only get you as far as the breakwater. But if you would leave the harbor to cross an ocean, you'll need a destination.

You'll need a purpose for your efforts.

So which is it?

Cicero once wrote, "... certain falsehoods impinge on all true statements." And in part, I think you make yourself these stories as a means to unearth the one you truly want to tell. Fiction, though untrue, allows us to experiment with virtue, with our morality, and it creates scenarios we don't have the luxury to let reality direct. And so we orchestrate situations to learn as much as we can about ourselves. To claim ownership of ourselves, because Fate's infatuation with control isn't about keeping it, but about pining for someone to relieve it of its burden.

Our whole dynamic shouldn't be like this. It shouldn't be me telling the story through you. It should be you telling the story through me. Does that even make sense? It sure sounds a lot like an oxymoron, or is it a paradox? Either way, it is you who should be in charge.

When will you take it?

When will you own yourself?

CHAPTER 41

You woke up on your last day in the hotel and decided to not board the ship.

You said you were done with it, that you had spent enough time away to not want to be away anymore.

And here we are, my friend, riffing on a page to see if some creative spark sets you on the right path, but with your mentality, as you are, blessings will sting like curses, fortunes will smack of burden, and the slightest itch will burn like rashes.

So what can we do?

How do we calm the shit show in your head?

Where else?

Where else, indeed, Orlando?

You go back to grandma.

CHAPTER 42

It had been years since the incident with the priest, and you'd heard she was doing business with a woman in Casco Viejo, a heavily gentrified sector of Panama City. You don't remember how you learned about this woman, but you knew of her.

You dropped everything and took the trip down to Panama. Your flight landed slightly after sunset. Twilight colored in the sky with reds and yellows and a fluid brushstroke of diaphanous green. It was hot and humid. A wave of heat washed and radiated down your face. Your ears itched. Your nose could smell itself. You didn't miss the weather.

The ride from the airport was long: little bursts of speed in between full stops. Traffic was terrible. You didn't miss this either, but the music on the radio was good. It had been a while since you listened to *bachata*. You'd forgotten its rousing effect on your mood. For a moment, you were almost cheerful. Then you made it to the *corredor*.

The *corredor* was the winding highway you remembered: cutting through destitute neighborhoods on the way to the city, faint lights traveling from zinc houses and many-colored homes along the hills. There was political propaganda along the road: the promise that nothing will ever change. Shopping malls up on the billboards: buy more and call it progress. For the country. For you!

Same dagger from another angle. Old anger from another source. The same slap on another cheek. And yet, it's not like you gave a shit. At least the food was great and there were restaurants everywhere. It's where you came from and so it felt like home regardless of what you thought of it. You could leave

Panama any time you wanted to, and this gave you the patience to love it.

The woman's name was Iloveny Castillo.

She was the kind of famous only certain people knew about. She was the kind of wealthy whose riches didn't necessarily grow but whose expenses steadily declined: a wealth nobody dared reduce. More than rich, she was powerful. And though nobody knows how, a few instants in her presence are enough to understand why: Iloveny is like a center of lower pressure, moving the very air to swirl in her direction, making the space around her heavy and unnatural, eery, almost, but humbling at the same time.

Her gaze made you feel like you'd get a tan from being exposed to it, her voice was crisp yet carried within itself a sort of echo. Her blinks were slow, and they reminded you of the ebb and flood of a powerful tide. In and out. Washing everything away. And you were but sand. And she was beautiful.

Shortly after you arrived she happened to be walking by. Hard to miss her, for sure. Iloveny Castillo was a tall, copper-skinned woman with luscious ebony hair undulating to her lower back. And she didn't happen to be walking by. She knew you were coming.

"Orlandito," she called, "how are you?"

"Fine, thank you, and you?" you said mechanically, reverting to the greeting you used to recite at teachers back in high school. You felt awkward. Reduced, even, to a child being caught redhanded or a starstruck fan.

Her smile was faint but it felt like laughter.

I took over.

I've done this several times.

You don't even notice, Orlando, because while half the time you're literally out of your mind, you're figuratively out of it the other half. You have a problem with escapism. And by problem I mean addiction. What you feared would happen if you ever did drugs happens more often than you think, and you owe more to me than you know, but I know how much you hate owing shit to people and I'm well aware how you can't distinguish gratitude from defeat. So, let's leave it at that, and calm the fuck down.

"There you are," she said. "Are you still letting the fleshy one take the helm?"

"I thought he could handle it."

"What is there to handle, Eu*daemon*?"

"You know not to use our names out loud."

"I do," she said, "that's why I do it. And you do remember what happens if you don't use mine back, right Euly?"

This time she laughed.

"Let's not get into this, Caco*daemon*."

"There you go. How am I to tell you apart, in any case? Unlike me, you've allowed Orlando to carry on perceiving."

"You know I go by Logos."

"Why haven't you taken over, then? While we're on the topic..."

"It isn't right."

"Isn't it, though? I mean I guess you *are* the good one, anyway."

"Am I? Historically, you've done more good than I have. I just haven't done anything bad."

"You *had* to bring up Socrates and Plato!"

"But you did so well back then, Iloveny. Look how much good has come from their work! I'll always be proud of you for that."

Picture it as you were asleep. I know it's a clichéd comparison but it is a lot like it, though you could say it's like daydreaming. You're not entirely unconscious. You're not plunged into oblivion, but you're not actively perceiving things.

Let me explain.

Sometime in the 1940s, the philosopher Gilbert Ryle

thought he'd go to town on Descartes' mind-body dualism theory, heavily criticizing it in his 1949 book *The Concept of Mind*.

Ryle aptly referred to our particular scenario as the 'ghost in the machine,' and he proposed Descartes' notion of the mind being separate from the brain was wrong, and rightly so.

With advances in neuroscience, it has been discovered that the brain is teeming with neurons and neurotransmitters, constantly moving information throughout the brain and nervous system. In turn, human identity, *You*, right now, is located somewhere in the prefrontal cortex, which can be divided into the medial prefrontal cortex, or mpfc, and the dorsal prefrontal cortex, dmpfc.

I *am* what Ryle would pejoratively dismiss as a ghost in the machine.

But I exist deeper still, on a shiftier plain: I exist within your *identity*.

But I do exist alongside your brain chemistry – albeit as a mere witness - yet I'm unaffected by your moods, passions, or desires. By *you*. If your body dies, and your identity shatters into nothing on the ether, I will go on existing. And with regards to the metaphysical portion of it all or, more to what you'll genuinely wonder, the eschatological aspect: don't ask: because I don't know. None of us do. All we know is we go from existing to oblivion and there is nothing in between.

We have no fixed qualities or gender.

You die, then I 'wake up' in someone else.

You never got around to watching *Ghost In The Shell*, by the way, which is a shame because you'd understand a little more of what I'm talking about, or it'd at least make you cool with it. But enough with all this.

Done.

Back to Iloveny.

That bitch!

I met her a long time ago, in Greece, as you probably gathered, but our existences haven't coincided since. I'm not sure if we always exist simultaneously, and I never thought to ask. For me, the mechanics of my existence don't matter. In a way, I'm immortal. And as long as there are complex identities that can host me, seeing as I've never found myself in an animal, I will go on as I have.

The only influence I can attribute to you is the fact I'm writing this, through you, meanwhile you think you're writing it through *me*, as with a muse.

Thing is, you'll never see these parts of the work. They will exist in the work much like I exist in tandem with you, and perhaps I'll read them in some distant future, through another pair of eyes, and I'll laugh to myself: a ghost in the page.

But, I continue to digress.

Iloveny!

The scum!

I do think Cacodae was involved with Descartes' on-point revelation and somehow managed to leak too much into his work, but I'll never know. Iloveny! This being under whom your grandmother utilized her gifts, however much it goes into charity (all of it).

Still!

This *daemon* has no care for human life.

But let's see what she's planned for us.

CHAPTER 43

You were twelve years old when *sensei* touched you.

But you still refrain from calling it abuse. You cower from the word 'molested.' But you were. And you avoid the words because you thought you were in control, but you weren't.

You've told yourself you didn't mind it much, which is preposterous, because at the time you certainly didn't like it. You tensed up. You felt embarrassed. Invaded. And you definitely minded his chapped, rough hand pressing into your skin to reach into your underwear.

You remember every pube tingling in disgust. You felt as if you wanted to pee, as if you wanted to run, as if you wanted, and you *wanted*, to escape.

But you couldn't.

He told you it was a special breathing technique and he would only teach it to you and you were oh so lucky – "my best student."

He told you he had to feel it with his fingers to make sure you got it right. He asked you to breathe harder, longer, with his whole hand down your groin, then he said you should breathe faster, as if you were running out of air, that it almost sounded like a gasp, with a bit of humming in between: he wanted you to moan.

He described it instead of asking because he knew you wouldn't know what a moan sounded like.

It was 1998.

He knew you were a child even as he did it because that is *why* he did it. And you obeyed. You did as he asked. You thought it was a new technique that would make you as strong as Goku and as strong as all the martial artists you admired, but this moment in space had only one victor. Because saying he won doesn't mean you lost. And though not all honesty is virtuous, hard facts are what you need right now.

Only one person was made bigger that day, and it was that devious, reprehensible pederast. Hell, even as you write this you almost feel as if you're lying. Part of you feels like you're making it up or making it sound worse than it was. Is this what fear sounds like? Is it shame? Is this denial? Are you in denial? Because it *happened*. It did. He touched you. He molested you. He succeeded. He got his way and walked away.

But he couldn't break you.

You're here.

And even though you've blocked it off and to this day are met with a blank space when you think of it, you did get over it. Because you know you had no fault in it.

And that's what matters.

CHAPTER 44

Let's dial back to your grandmother before we go on to Iloveny and her antics.

She called when you went out for a walk. Your phone was off. Time flowed faster in your mind.

It was one of those days where you could see the moon at noon, in autumn, as the trees swooned with a thousand shades of fire. The wind was temperate; the lake rippled into vibrant, undulating wavelets. The silence peppered with rustling leaves and the low beats of water against the rocks, of peace amidst life.

You were in New Hampshire.

You were home.

Then winter came. Lovely, heavenly winter.

Red and gold aged to pearly whites, a silver breeze: pure, alabaster paradise. And you felt like dancing. You felt like breathing. You felt free because you were invisible in the blizzard, and you walked to the middle of the lake and took your clothes off: your jacket, your shirt, and as you stood there naked the air flowed around you laden in frost and snow and mountain chill. You opened your arms and in that moment felt your skin quiver under the tender nibble of the breeze, your breath smoking out your teeth into clouds of revelry and relief – and have you ever been surrounded by a storm? The cold air slowing down your blood – and have you ever been hugged by the world itself? Felt the jealous tug of gravity against the yearning gale? Have you ever smiled that wide? Or been so enraptured?

Not once had you stood amidst a space devoid of all but you. It was freeing. It felt good. The solitude.

And that's okay.

You looked *so* happy!

And I was, too.

When you got back in the house, your grandmother called.

Last you spoke was when you left a few days after the priest's visit. This was right before you were due onboard. She said she'd like to finish the story, and she was wondering if you got home alright. You had, and she went on.

You remember how at first she was apprehensive, how she would hold things back, thinking you would judge her or see her differently, but once she realized you were listening, genuinely listening, she began to speak more freely.

"There isn't much left from where we left off to when you were born," she said, though you knew that was a space of twenty-three years and surely there were points of note.

And yet, that was for her to decide. And she chose not to share.

"I've lived through minutes that felt longer than months, *lijo*," she said, "and so I'll leave those years in the same dust into which they turned."

"After your uncle was born," she explained, "things with your grandfather worsened."

You hummed for her to go on.

"The details don't matter. Well, they do, but I won't discuss them because they have been mine to endure, and I do not wish to revisit them. Things got bad. Then they were neutral. Tolerated. And then things were fine. Now, we're here."

"I see," you said. "We don't have to talk about it, grandma. I understand."

"I know you do, *lijo*. You've grown a lot. I can see that. You've had your own experiences since you were but a child running around here terrified of the dark."

You remembered.

You used to run away as soon as you turned off the lights in a room, picturing pale faces reaching out with bony fingers to do who-knows-what to you. Your fear of the dark isn't fully gone, though, albeit placated by the years.

I'm surprised to hear you ever feared the dark at all. Now you even make a habit of going into a room and shutting off the lights. You figure in the dark there's nothing and you're nowhere, and this means you could be anywhere. Anyone. Anything. But I do know why you don't fear it anymore. All the monsters you've met have fucked with you in the light. You've learned shit doesn't lurk around and jump at you: it's there where you can see it, you often walk right into it, and all you wield is that dumb smile on your face.

There's no catch.

Only you, and me.

"I'm not afraid anymore," you said.

"I know."

A year went by and the last you spoke with her was that. She allowed you the aspect of her story she felt comfortable sharing. And she hoped it was enough. And it was. The next time you shipped it was under querulous circumstances. You had been out of a job for a long time, looking around and spitting out resumes to see what bit. I suppose nothing wants to bite spit, but so came the metaphor, incidentally, like spit.

I could write that you learned a lot from shipping, but every experience is but an opportunity, and opportunity without attention is just passing time. An experience is nothing if you don't observe it. The lessons aren't granted but rather relative. You learn because you observe, and you observe because you've honed your mind to be receptive.

It worked for you. You absorbed. From everything, and everyone: how to be and how not to be.

You had never been to Ecuador. You had never worked in Ecuador, let alone onboard a petroleum-product tanker ship. The entire trip was an experience, and like all experiences, it was laced with the good and the bad aspects of life. The conditions of the ship weren't what you were used to, certainly, and the crew wasn't exactly familiar.

You had never been 'one of the boys,' and this being the primary mode of shipboard relationships, of Latin American relationships, at least as far as you had seen, you were consequently worried of how it would turn out. You'd had no time to formulate an adequate persona, which is how you've dealt with new environments in the past and, ironically, however much you've criticized your previous workplace, you had space to be yourself most times.

As Albert Camus wrote in his novel *The Stranger*, "After a while, you could get used to anything." And you did. The inconveniences of the living conditions soon became laughing points, and you didn't mind them much. The fact you didn't have any bedsheets or linen was quickly solved by some T-shirts tied up into a sheet. The cold air-conditioning, which you much preferred to clammy heat, was ameliorated by tying up a coverall's legs and using it as a sleeping bag. The pillow was a shirt stuffed with underwear. You constantly washed and rotated what you wore, and your towel was whichever shirt you had used throughout the day. You were also not getting paid much, so it was really a trip made for the sea-time.

And you did get used to it.

You came face to face with your biases. You learned you assumed the worse in people, and they weren't always as bad as you'd imagined. You did nothing to fit in because there should be no need for it. Any place where you need to 'fit into' isn't worth the effort. There are so many kind and positive people out there, and so you shouldn't have to tolerate those who aren't. You learned to do you. To focus on you. And welcome anyone who reaches out sincerely. Shut out anyone with even the slightest hint of pretense. Because there is neither the need nor the time for any of it.

There were stretches of tedium punctuated by marvelous sights: a quiet sunset as a stingray leapt over the sun, a rainbow pushing through a cloud, mountain ranges flat-and-spiking like heartbeats in the distance. You counted five shooting stars within an hour. After dinner: the green flash of twilight. The sky dressed in fire. Each day was made up of as much loneliness as of wonder. And it was good. It was fine.

A sailor's adage speaks of stars glowing brighter at sea, "they know only the worthy are out there to see them." A bold claim, certainly, with the specious self-righteousness of your average seafarer, but still: the stars *were* brighter.

And it didn't matter for whom or why – because it was beautiful.

CHAPTER 45

Iloveny called it her 'pocket of existence.'

It was midnight, and I kept the reigns of flesh as long as we were near her, to be safe, and you watched on.

There was a red door in a dilapidated wall. It looked condemned.

A massive Corotú tree rose lavishly over a courtyard worthy of hosting the best of fairy tales. The Corotú was regal. Portentous. Built so massive that its branches were as thick as oak trees, whose bark may be older than the city: all held in place by a trunk as proud as the centuries it has enjoyed in growth and power.

I felt it through you: the humbling feeling of standing before a living thing that would certainly outlast you. Perhaps this is how one feels about children, but the terrifying possibility of it not being the case extinguishes the humility of it.

But enough of that!

Iloveny's weekly bacchanalia is famous, though it's uncertain if she means once a week or a week long, and it was in fullswing as we came in.

"You should come and see," she said. "I'd like to see your face."

"What for?"

"It's been ages since I've seen you scared."

It wasn't what I expected.

The mood was placid instead of rowdy, the air was cool and almost sweet with myrrh and laughter. There was a breeze flowing through the windows and down into the courtyard. The décor was rustic yet refined, kept so by a team of artisans dedicated to every inch of the interior. The furniture was exquisite; the decorations emblematic; the music… *that* is what struck me the most.

They came in their folkloric dress and glided to the center courtyard as it were a stage, or more as if whatever space their feet touched morphed into a theater. I could swear I caught the sunflowers crane to face the stage.

A silence befell. A tremor was felt. The breeze: wasn't there.

"We can stay for the rehearsal if you'd like," she whispered to me.

"Won't that spoil the performance?"

"The Kokua never repeat a performance, even if it was only a rehearsal."

"So they improvise?"

"In a way, yes."

"So why rehearse if they always improvise?"

"They rehearse as a form of training, not practice. Creativity tends toward decay. Much like the body, if left unexercised and unstimulated, it withers and becomes feeble. It fails. It grows mold and festers until it eats at you inside, and there's no getting it back in shape."

"Sounds like a lot of work."

"It is, and yet when you see them on stage, it's as if they had been holding their breath and have at last begun to breathe. It isn't a job for them, you see, it's a calling. A vocation."

We came upon a large lime-green, wooden door from some Celtic dream. She pushed it open, faintly, it felt invasive, as if the slightest noise were a garish imposition.

The doors closed behind us, anachronistic metal arms pushing them in easy patience as we gazed into the courtyard.

The moon filtered the sun's fire to a soothing glimmer of nebulous light. A dim radiance dripped from the moving air, and the sky was curious, peeking and sneaking a glance for this single moment. And we stood in eager attendance. The musicians were ready, forming a wide circle with their instruments.

A clap was heard.

A man came forth bedecked in the traditional dress, hand-made by a talent only matched by the performance for which it was sewn. He moved slowly, but it looked as if the world flowed behind him while he stood still.

He looked up and aimed his gaze at me. And I mean at *me*, inside of *you*, as if he *knew*.

He cleared his throat.

> *El cielo llueve sobre la tierra,*
> *Sin nubes ni avisos ni vergüenza,*
> *El mundo dormido le pregunta,*
> *"Por qué has de llover hoy?"*
> *El cielo le contesta señalando a los hombres,*
> *"Hoy no lluevo pero te escupo,*
> *"Mira la inmundicia que has dejado crecer!"*

He paused, looked up, and turned quickly with a scream that, somehow, left no echo in the air, as if it could only be heard once. Magical – I could think of no other word – how magical was his display! Perhaps my dramatic sense made it all grander than it was, but, by inexistent God! It was glorious.

> *Un día el Silencio reposaba en un prado,*
> *Cuando la Mente le huye a la Conciencia.*
> *Sin saber, el Silencio la invita,*
> *"Ven aquí, hermana, siéntate conmigo."*
> *La Conciencia se oía a lo lejos,*
> *Y la Mente, temblorosa, le contesta de reojo,*
> *"Hermana, gracias,*
> *"Pero si estoy contigo, me alcanza la Conciencia."*

Again he turned, swiftly, the tenor of his voice surging from his lungs into my ears. He thrust his staff against the ground and continued.

En algún reflejo del amanecer,
Sobre el rostro de una mujer,
Una gota de sangre conoce a una lágrima.
La lágrima le pregunta,
"Sangre, tú qué haces por ella cuando fluyes?"
La sangre le responde,
"Yo, Lágrima, cuando fluyo la mantengo viva.
"Y tu, qué haces cuando fluyes?"
La lágrima sonríe y le contesta,
"En vez, Sangre, mi flujo es prueba que está viva."

There were no curtains closing or thundering applause. It was quiet as they walked into the backroom.

"It's offensive to applaud," Iloveny explained.

"Why?"

"They believe their performance allows Nature to speak through them. They feel a connection with all things, at least that's how they explained it. The *Kokua* don't perform for people, Eugy, they pay tribute to Nature and its gifts. To applaud would make it human. They'd have you greet them with a hush and let their words soar in peace up to the spirits. They'd have the awe of your silence, not the presumption of your praise."

"It was a beautiful performance, Cacodae," I said, making sure to speak her name.

"They always are."

We walked to another courtyard.

"I want to show you something," she said.

As we entered, the wooden building shook as if dancing along. I was too far to hear the music or get the words; it was too dark, where I was, to see the dancing, but the whole building echoed the performance, a faint recall of its twists. It had an inescapable, methodical rhythm that shook the place as if directed by a phantom metronome.

It was a Spanish-style courtyard with a tall brick wall with glass windows in the background. A cordon of enthralled viewers surrounded the performance in a circle - a stage made by people that from above looked like some ancient ritual - and over to the side the music was played by an old lady and a creepy-looking teenager.

It was a playful performance, a tonal revamping from the performance I'd seen before.
This one brimmed with joy. It was exuberant. Iloveny's assistants raised a hand at her arrival and everything stopped.

"Good evening," she said. "I'd like to introduce my friend Euly. Give him a warm welcome!"

We went down an imperial, carpeted staircase towards the courtyard. The music resumed and the dancing regained its course.

"This is part of our Pun Series," she said. "Each group was asked to write a poem with a pun. This was the winner."

The spectacle swayed the building once again, and the cohort of viewers in the audience began clapping to the rhythm of the drums. A young girl began chanting:

> *Father Time had a bastard child named Nick.*
> *And Nick would perform many deeds,*
> *Good and evil, at precisely the right time.*
>
> *He'd stoke the flame when heretics were burned;*
> *He'd swing the noose whenever slaves were hung;*
> *He'd waft the scent of flesh from the furnace to the tyr*
> *ant;*
> *He's always been around, just and precisely.*
>
> *Nick is the confession that is overheard,*
> *The lingering fragrance of the one you love,*
> *The silent instigator of the ocean storm.*
> *He's the impulse of a bird,*

The resistance of the glide,
The fierce tugging against gravity
From a hurricane's pride.

Nick, you see, is a deity of the air,
A presence of propitious time,
A child of Father Time and the Goddess of the Wind.

But nowadays he whispers in the small:
He blows the candle before the child,
Knocks the beer-can before it's done.
He tells the world when you're in love,
And hears the smile behind the door.

Nick is always there,
At the perfect time,
When conditions are ideal and right before they're gone.
He made that time his own,
And his father let him have it.
It has become, since…
The Nick of Time.

I didn't expect any of the things I saw. I expected yet another of her trademark evenings. Revelry, yes, but depravity, too. I expected laughter, sure, but perversion as the cause. Malice. Indulgence. I was surprised. And she gloated over it.

Another wave to her staff and the performance was about to start.

The lights dimmed; various torches lit up the dance floor. Silence grew. Anticipation consumed all who watched. There was a full moon. The spectral glare of lunar rays poured into the courtyard as a slow, improvised percussion challenged the stillness. From previous performances, I had seen their scorn for the metronome. Music, the way they make it, and dance, the way they manifest it, are slaves to no structure.

The percussion intensified. I wasn't sure if it was the strength or the speed or the aftermath of some deeper skill, but it was a metronome in itself, ironically, to which our heartbeats slowed and sped in tune.

The first dancer walked in. I could hear the torches burn. Full-on display, yet so innocuously, he stood at the center of the stage and all sound was his. The drums echoed on his breath, the very air was aversive to his space. All eyes on him – I could hear the moonlight sizzle on his skin - he looked up, slammed his staff across acoustics that could not be real, and spoke:

> *Me dijo del mono*
> *Que sus gritos son sordos,*
> *Y del pulpo*
> *Que su gloria se encuentra en las nubes.*
> *Me dijo de las aves*
> *Que sus sueños rezan bajo las aguas,*
> *Y que en mi existencia no se alcanza la dicha.*
> *Me dijo que mis cuentos son alas efímeras,*
> *Y que el humano*
> *En su arrogancia*
> *Cree que es versátil.*
> *Me dice que las musas mueren de hambre,*
> *Que sus alimentos se marchitan,*
> *Por mentes sin sangre*
> *Que engendran ilusiones sin vida.*

The music exploded around him.

Ten if not a dozen players now surrounded him. He looked up, slammed his staff, and all sound stopped right before the last note of his thud. I heard it.

The synchronicity was astounding.

Iloveny raised her hand with a bell and made a single strike, held it with her finger so it didn't manage to swing back.

He looked up, didn't use the staff, but spoke:

> *Me dice que mi piel morena es por camuflaje,*
> *Que bajo la tierra desnudo los gusanos no me encuentran,*
> *Que mi dulzura los empalaga,*

Y que si los gusanos fuesen monos nadie los escucha.
Me cuenta que el pulpo fue en búsqueda de las nubes,
Y que el ave,
Desde un árbol,
Le pidió diez cuentos del mundo bajo las aguas.
Al fin, me dijo que lo efímero no es siempre fantasía,
Y que de ilusiones hay mil canciones.
He aquí, entonces,
La milésima estrofa,
De mis arrogantes ilusiones.

A sliver of darkness held the lights at bay, as he walked off the stage in the waning shadow of the moonlight's glare. I have no idea how they planned it, or if coincidence rose to add drama to the stage. But it was marvelous.

Iloveny stood next to me with a smile. She paid me no heed. She was enamored with the performance.

As was I.

I slept that night dreaming about it. So deeply so, that you took back the flesh.

And so it began.

CHAPTER 46

At first you noticed the little things.

As you do.

You hate soft beds, always favoring the rock-hard beds you first experienced in China, and so you knew you hadn't consciously chosen that bed over the Japanese one right next to it.

The sun came in brightly.

White sheets and curtains mustered up a glare. Your eyes strained. You sat up and looked around you. There was water on the nightstand. Lemons. Some lavender. The taste of ass in your mouth. I'd forgotten to brush your teeth.

I did nothing. I stayed put. I let you see things for yourself, mainly because I felt guilty for taking over. You were yet to speak to me. You knew I was quiet. You felt I was ashamed, and you let it be.

Whatever you may think, we don't control each other, and the only reason I was able to take over was that you didn't know I could.

I had saved it for when it was necessary, spiritually necessary, like meeting another *daemon*. But I could feel your resentment. I knew it made you angry not because I did it without your permission, but because there had been innumerable times when you would've willingly conceded.

There had been times when it would've been nice to enjoy the bliss of suicide without having died or succumbed to drugs.

"You let me suffer through all that," you finally said, "knowing you could have helped."

But I couldn't have, Orlando, because I shouldn't have.

And no, it's not a rule, or a law, and it is no god's edict

which imposed this normative on us. It was *me.* I chose to let you suffer the hits because I needed you to be strong. I couldn't save you because if I did you wouldn't be able to save me when it came to it. And you can now.

You're hurt, Orlando, but *fuck* are you not fucking *capable?* You're on your way to face a *daemon*, Caco*daemon*, and look at you walk your steps dauntlessly. I mean, look at yourself! I don't regret shit.

You knew she'd be in the library because it was the only room with its doors wide open. She was sitting by the window. She'd always liked the drama of a well-poised scene. She welcomed you with a smile, directed you to a table she'd readied with all of your worldly pleasures.

There was tea: matcha, Pu'er, and yerba mate. Temperature-controlled kettles ready to heat richly alkalized water to seventy-five degrees Celsius or a scalding boil. There were snacks: dried mangoes, cashew nuts, root vegetable chips, and even dried squid. Pies of matcha-chocolate *gateau.* Multi-Green kombucha. Mochi galore.

She had a bottle of Ardbeg Ten and one of Bruichladdich Octomore. An assortment of bitter New England IPA's and – I could go on – everything your tongue had learned to associate with happiness.

The library was filled with books. There was there smell of dust and old paper – of *vellichor* - that you've been obsessed with since you'd taken a passion for reading, paired with the faint hint of freshly cut grass and malted peat. How she did it doesn't matter, but your senses were enraptured.

She came at you smiling, with her easy grace of beautiful *everything.* A sway of natural cheer and charm, her eyes a brilliant amber glinting under eloquent eyebrows cradling all of her wit. A smirk on rich lips, plump with coquetry and kind and tender. A triumph, an epitome: a manifestation of anything and everything conceivably gorgeous. She was it. All of it. Beauty, to its entirety. And yes, yet again, your senses were enraptured.

This was the moment for me to be in control. But you

wouldn't let me. Why would you? She knew what she was doing. She always has. Iloveny was your idealized embodiment of perfection. Inside *and* out. But I wasn't about to let you succumb, my friend.

I've seen you down this path and stood by and let you take the hits because I knew you'd make it through, painfully, catastrophically, but through.

But you weren't strong enough to turn your back on Iloveny. Nobody is. Not even me. We were trapped.

Until your grandmother came in.

CHAPTER 47

It had been years since you last saw your grandmother.

She was dressed in traditional *Kokua* garb. A white tunic, with colored triangles stitched in symmetrical rows from neck to toes, entirely made from the *Pulsenia Armata* tree. She looked regal. Her expression grim yet somehow tender. Her eyes were tense, her lips relaxed, she held her hands behind her back as she approached, and she hugged you like she did the priest.

It all went blank.

You thought of how it took you hours to get over picking a sock then picking which foot would wear one first. You remembered when your ankle got stuck on your bike when you were five years old and it dug a hole in it. You remember your mother rubbing brown sugar in it. You thought of the man you killed in Huadu. You remembered the morning you woke up in a bathroom in Shanghai. You thought of *sensei* groping down your groin while asking you to moan.

You thought of the times you opened up to someone and realized there were few. You thought of how your sister taught your parents the emotional intelligence you wished they had when you were a child.

The times you woke in the middle of the night and didn't kill yourself.

When you realized you never wanted death but for someone to convince you to live.

Because you needed persuasion, you needed a reason, a purpose, or at least someone to blame for it.

You thought of all the gods you didn't believe in, and the one you did, once, by pretense: of the time you fabricated stories in front of a congregation. You blatant, narcissistic fuck! You remembered jumping into the river in La Mesa, the winds hushing the world in Patagonia, the ecstasy of an evening walk in Tokyo. Falling in love with your wife's liberty. The Hawaiian Islands. Diamond Head. Ramen shops. Used bookstores. And the fact none of it helped you hold down happiness. None of it endured the onslaught of depression. Of hatred.

You shouted my name and were met with silence. You thought of when you walked by a conversation and they were talking vices: of lust, and alcohol, of money. In passing you were asked what yours was and you said, "Solitude."

You thought perhaps you wanted to sound deep, but the more you thought of it you realized how true it was. How right you were. How much you're like the mimosa plant, closing shut as soon as something touches you.

Solitude is peace. But solitude can be a vice, too, because you want too much of it, and it's never enough.

Solitude is a vice, too, because you want it all the time, even when you shouldn't, even against your will, to the detriment of sanity and despite whom it may hurt, at the expense of growth and the patience of those who love you.

But solitude can also be a virtue, because despite the drift to hate yourself, you've learned to love your company.

It's normal, even in a relationship with yourself, to be but sand beneath the tide of love and hate. Back and forth.

The echoes of all your conversations rung inside your ears and you could hear yourself screaming, yelling yourself into existence, shouting out to summon what little pleasures had made you real throughout the years, a focus of perception, a particle from superposition.

You felt yourself muster, materialize, to manifest: a swift wind roiling in the distance, enveloping the clustered noise of all your memories and fusing them with the crowded cries of all your reasoning into a single, molded pebble of despair.

And how much can the human heart take? How much can

it take as it hones in on itself, bites down on itself, and plumbs from its self-hatred the skill to finally love itself?

And how much truth is left in memory as it filters through resentment? Through nostalgia? And the noise, the noise, the screams, the soothing music, and the flash of colors nameless and the shrieks, the cries, and the smiles in between the laughter as you shake inside and think of all the things you fucked up for vain sake of misery and art and the forest blooming green and the leaves turning red fiery red and the frost calming everything down and you no longer saw the moon at noon and no chipmunks ran around the trees and the winds rose up into the sky lifting the snow from the frozen lake and the noise, the noise, the loud, raucous banging of your mind against your heart and the dreams you dreamt at night against what crept during the day as you tried oh so hard to not think, to not think, to not think about all the pain paired with all the voices your eyes tried to overhear and your skin prickled at the sound, the vibrations, the energy that made your teeth clatter against themselves.

And you're floating.

Hovering above your face.

Everything goes white then it goes black: a void.

A warm pressure over your body. You feel like a piece of clay inside a sculptor's hand, inside a poet's mind.

Light, caring pressure. Intent, dedicated hope.

A hushed, vacuous life.

The abyss.

And your grandmother's embrace.

And then there was me: standing above silence, a negligence in time and empty space. Greeting you: looking like you. An idealized, unreachable version of you. I spoke like you. I stood like you. I was you.

We met at last.

You spoke first, remember?

***

Her hug induced a state of *Epoché*, a rightfully coveted philosophical state.

It comes from the Greek word ἐποχή, which roughly means 'cessation' or a 'suspension of belief.'

The term emerged in ancient Greece during the Hellenistic Period as the staple argument of Academic Skepticism under Pyrrho. More importantly, it came to your attention when you were reading about existentialism in *At The Existentialist Café*, by Sarah Bakewell, and as you read it struck you as coincidental, because at the time a state of *epoché* was exactly what you needed.

But you needed more than forgetfulness.

You needed a hard reset. You wanted a state of nothing, so you could finally assess the bits of *something* that you had allowed into your mind. And what did we find there, Orlando?

Some shit…

Some shit we found.

We found all of the emotions you repressed as a child. The times you believed fear was cowardice, that nerves were for the weak, and that arrogance was the same as confidence. We found a swamp of unwept tears, stagnant and green with vermin of the worst kind. Black mold festered in your eyes.

Because males are strong. Men don't cry and they sure as shit don't talk about their feelings. Men cull. Men are rational. Men are strong.

Strong!

And men shouldn't feel anything because if they do they might break and what's the use, what's the point, we say, of a broken man? A useless creature with no yield. Is that the word? To yield? To produce? To function and brew utility?

Well, fuck *that*.

In Japan, buildings are built to be flexible and absorb shock. Seismic movements are assimilated and redirected. An immovable object can still break. Against a strong enough force, a steel heart is no different from glass. Hard shatters. Flexible stands. Let's stand, man.

It's okay.

It's okay.

It's okay if you're not alright, as long as it's willful growth that follows, as long you line the cracks in gold to weld yourself shut.

Feel, man.

Men feel.

You can feel.

Epoché was hard at first. Oblivion is no joke. You always pictured it would be a white expanse of nothing, but it was black.

It was anything.

It was a storm of wind wrapping your essence and floating in the void.

You sensed nothing.

Then there was the deafening noise of wind gusts in your ears. The shifty embrace of gales pounding at your body, from every direction, keeping you in place as if by dynamic positioning. You thought of the lake in New Hampshire.

You tried to find yourself.

To hone into yourself.

But without memory, there is no self.

Without a story, there is no character.

There is only what comes before the story, before the memories, before the self: the *daemon.*

"Hello," I said.

CHAPTER 48

"I figured you'd look like me," you said.

"I don't."

"I know, but still…"

"Still what?"

"It's nice to talk to myself," you said.

"I know."

"Are you almost finished writing?" I asked

"Are you?"

"I think so."

"I've got a bit more to go."

"Will I get to read it?"

"You know you won't," I said.

"Ever?"

"Ever."

"What's the point, then?"

"It's for me."

"The future you?"

"In a way."

"Posterity?"

"I guess."

"Fame?"

"What fame? There's only two of us."

"Two of you at a time," you said, "but many more before and after."

"It's still only us."

"You know, I pictured this conversation a lot differently."

"What did you expect, Orlando? Some deep philosophical discourse? A treatise on existence and nervous turmoil? You should know better by now."

"I know you're right, but still. It's a bit anticlimactic."

You laughed.

"There needn't be a climax," I said. "If there were one there is no reason it should be now. This isn't a destination, you know."

"Then what the fuck is it? I'm literally inside my head speaking with the embodiment of my consciousness. What else is there?"

"I don't know. I don't even know where we're going with this. I'm sure later on we will think of better ways we could've spent this opportunity. More fruitful uses for this time. But shit happens like this and we're never ready. You know this. Fortune strikes and we have no fucking clue what to do with it, and we end up wasting it. Why should this be any different? Why should we not waste this chance trying to 'make the best of it' instead of living in it, randomly, and perhaps thinking back on it ruefully, nostalgically, I could hope, and let stuff happen as it would? Why do we have to control *everything*? It's tiring! I'm exhausted, Orlando, even I, of thinking about everything. Look at this! Us, in a state of *epoché,* and somehow we're paradoxically overthinking things."

"Will it be done once she lets go?"

"Yes."

"And all I got to do was get to meet myself, then?"

"I suppose."

"Some would say it wasn't a waste after all, then."

"I'd say it wasn't."

"So would I, man."

CHAPTER 49

Your breathing was even.

Paced.

And your eyes opened slowly as if from a deep sleep.

She stood over you.

Iloveny.

Iloveny, wearing your grandmother's face. And the realization didn't strike you at first. It was beyond me, too, until long after I realized and told you.

It felt as if your mind was held within a soft, floating vessel of air surrounded by a water dam: holding all of your thoughts, and all possible interpretations your identity gave to those thoughts.

Every iteration of you was mustered behind those walls, waiting to flood the wispy valley of silence your grandmother's hug had given you.

But perhaps it's the wrong analogy, because it wouldn't come like a flood.

It wouldn't happen all at once. It'd begin with a trickle and a slow pouring. You'd see it happen. Your thoughts and biases making their way back into your mind, behind your eyes, and you'd think there was a long time left, a long time left before it all comes back and so you should enjoy the valley a little longer before you act with the limber mind the *epoché* had given you.

But it'd be too late when you decide to act.

It happens to everyone, as it happened to you, and the state of *epoché* is more a drug than an advantage, you see, much like it would be to take opium or morphine, but without the physical addiction. Without dependency.

Iloveny knew this could be monetized, so she did.

If Iloveny could stand there looking like your grandmother, holding you, it meant only one thing.

I'm sorry, Orlando.

I'm sure you know it, too.

What I don't know is *when* she died, and which portion of your memories of her is actually Iloveny – *Cacodaemon* – and which portion is truly your grandmother.

And I'm not sure you'd want to know.

*****

"When did she die?" you asked her. "Is this fucking real? She's dead?"

"Not yet," Iloveny said. "Not now."

"Where is she?"

"Would you like to talk to her?"

"Yes!"

There wasn't a grand display of shifting light beams or shaking water cups. There was barely a blink and then there was your grandmother, smiling. She didn't look lost or concerned, but you could tell she knew what happened.

"Grandma?" you asked.

"Hola, *lijo*."

"What is all this?"

"She showed up to the house one day."

"And you let her in?"

"You know it's normal for people to stop by unannounced in La Mesa, *lijo*. Some people want a meal, some want the conversation, and others want silence and a chair. I don't have much, *lijo*, but I've always managed to have all of those things and what's even better: I've always managed to not need much else."

"And then what happened?"

"She explained who she was. Said she was a *daemon* and she was looking for a host."

"A host for what?"

"She said I had a soothing effect on people, and if I let her she could help me help more people."

"The hug?"

"Yes," she said, "do you remember when I first did it with the priest?"

"Yes, I do. It was amazing."

"It was, wasn't it? And I've done it with many people since, as I've done it with you right now. It's a marvelous feeling, right?"

"Yes. It is, grandma, but - "

"But I enjoy it, too. People breathe differently. Their hearts slow down. I hear their minds pulsating a lullaby. And though I do see what they see at first, all the flashing memories soaring in their minds before the silence happens, though I feel what they feel as if it had happened to me, I enjoy it. Because many times I would've loved to have someone understand how I felt, and when they wake up they see I understand them. And it feels good."

You could see she was happy.

You smiled, and she smiled at you.

"Have you tried hugging yourself to see what happens?" you asked.

"You know, I never have. Is that strange?"

"I suppose it's common, especially for you."

"Well, it's not like other people can do what I do with a hug."

"Can't they?"

You looked at each other. Neither of us remembers if it was still morning or if noon already scorched around the town, but there was daylight and the threat of rain in the distance. The sound of waves and parakeets.

"I don't have long, *lijo*."

She said it casually, like it made no difference.

"You don't have long with these abilities?"

"To live, *lijo*. You know what I meant."

"I know."

CHAPTER 50

Before we go on, think of what you read in Merleu-Ponty's *Phenomenology of Perception.*

It's appropriate because, whether we talk about your profession or your life, the principle still applies.

When you're maneuvering a ship, it's all about migrating fixity. The entire process is an act of proprioception, the body's ability to perceive its position in space. It's also known as *kinaesthesia*, and it's made possible by mechanosensory neurons located within your muscles, tendons, and joints. It allows for you to point exactly at your nose when your eyes are closed.

Try it!

This same proprioception has been proven to extend to objects we manipulate, like swords, bats, a car, and in your case: a ship. The object is suffused by 'extended proprioceptors' that allow you to manipulate it effectively, subconsciously knowing exactly where it ends and where it begins.

Do you not think it's amazing you go around an entire day driving a car over seventy miles per hour from point A to point B without so much as touching *anything?*

On a ship, it helped you picture that your proprioceptors coated the whole vessel, and from that point on you got better, because it gave you the so-called 'feel' for the ship.

It wasn't salty magic bestowed by the ocean gods, Orlando. It's science. It's a skill. And you can hone it.

Every aspect of a maneuver requires fixity, a point from which to gauge the movement of each extremity on the ship: the bow lined up with a far-off rock, the stern against an edge of black mold growing on a building. Anything works as long as it bears fixity: as long as you can use it as a reference. You remove and apply forces to produce and counter-produce resultants. In your head: time, and evolving vectors.

A maneuver is an exercise of the intellect, a keen observance of growing patterns to calculate a singular, executive reaction. And this same mental model can be applied to personal behavior.

To *your* behavior.

Fixity doesn't mean constancy. Your point of reference need not be the same in every situation. It's about Migrating Fixity. There's a different reference for every portion of the action, for every decision, and every point in your existence.

It can change when you need it to change.

Your idea of your grandmother, which in reality was your idea of *you* because of how she made you feel about yourself, has been the point of fixity throughout this entire journey.

But now it has migrated without you knowing.

An unexpected force has been applied.

And what do good ship-handlers do in this situation?

They adapt.

They act.

The best advice you ever got about piloting is that the ship is not in charge. You are. A pilot never waits and sees. A pilot takes action.

Life isn't in charge either, my friend. You are. So handle it.

Handle yourself.

Own yourself!

CHAPTER 51

She died in her sleep.

She died before you could find out if it was her whom you remembered or what you had idealized her to be. You wondered if she'd be sad, if she'd be hurt to know you didn't get to know the real her but settled for an idea of her. You wondered if it was a betrayal. Or if it was laziness.

You thought maybe it wasn't your fault. With me 'taking over' and Iloveny messing around with your grandmother, how could you have known who you were, let alone who she was. But you must always wonder who you are. If you've never wondered who you are, it means you have been told, and you have accepted it.

You would remain an archetype, a type of person, and never go on to evolve into an individual. A personality. Indivisible.

It's good you finally asked yourself this, though you've always known the difference between who you are and whom you've had to be to get through the day. You cling to that difference because it keeps who you are alive, never mistaking it for the one you've been made to create.

As for your grandmother, it's hard to tell.

For you, at least. Because for her, she had always been certain of who she was. There was always a certainty in her eyes, a steady cadence to her words, up to her last moments, even after all she had seen and lived: she had a stalwart grip of herself.

I don't blame you for not knowing.

And neither would she.

****

It must've been hard to see her on that bed.

After all those years, after what you experienced through her the day before she died, after seeing how Iloveny wore her like a dress and then dumped her on the bed like clothes ready to be folded and put away. I can't imagine how you must've felt.

I mean it, too: I can't.

Once I take over your body I create a rupture between us, and because of this I no longer have access to your thoughts and feelings anymore, which is sad.

And this is why I'd never done it before. There was too much to lose. But now it's done.

Iloveny came to you at noon, back in her nymph-like persona, a glimmering of everything you'd find lovely. She put her hand on your shoulder and asked to be followed. She had something to show you.

"A black, tilted lighthouse," she said, "barely clinging to a rock," by southern entrance to the Panama Canal.

I said a lot of things to get you to stay. I did. But you heard none of it.

"Oh, the things you shall see!" she said. "After all, truths are best shown than told."

****

The door opened into a booth.

It was clear glass all over. Dark. The door was more a hatch than a door. You went in, it closed, you sat, and the booth went on.

The view opened into a landscape, but it wasn't tropical. It reminded you of Vancouver. It reminded you of Osaka. But it was neither, and it certainly wasn't Panama. There was a city and a harbor. Mountains. Mist and rivers.

The booth went on.

Tall buildings cowered into stumps, roads and highways

sunk like trenches in the distance, and the sunset, as you rose, held a green, steady glimmer in the twilight.

You looked behind you, and far off, over a bed of mist roiling on the horizon, the snow flowed liquid down the mountains like rivers of waking summer. The mist made the peaks look as if they floated in the sky, and in the wind, there was a tune: a bit of the snooze of winter, maybe the yawn of spring, there was a soothing whisper choiring with the birds.

It could've been the wiring. The winch. Whatever lifted the booth. Whatever it was, it brought a quaking breathlessness to your chest, even if the landscape didn't make any sense.

"It's beautiful, isn't it?" she said. "And what's best: you will not age as long as you're in this lighthouse."

You were young, and still thought time was equitable with life...

"Does that mean I'll never die?" you asked her.

If only you could see it as I see it...

"All physical decay stops," she explained, "your body will continue to regenerate cells as fast as it did when you entered here. You won't die, but you can be killed."

You think of your life as either a brooding or choleric chase for purpose. Ever a denizen of the extremes... I did try to be your balance...

"I get to live, then, for eternity?"
"As long you as you stay in here, yes."

I hoped in time you'd learn from things that live in the slow-passing: the melting glacier, the eroding mountain, the fading star... Trust me, eternity is nothing but a slow trot to suicide.

She put her hand on your shoulder. It was heavy. Her eyes affixed to yours. Her lips were steady. Her breath in tune with the air. You had never felt so real, so dense, so utterly perceived.

"So," she said, "what do you think?"

***

You arrived at a library: a tall, slim, cylindrical edifice with a vaulted ceiling.

People were walking around in random clothing, there was no palette of colors. The place was flecked with a myriad niches and pockets of eclectic décor, as if sprinkled by the shaking of a brush. A kaleidoscope of color. But not a sound was heard.

There was a weightless, breezy energy flowing through the air, somehow, even with people everywhere. Everyone walked silently. Sounds flowed along the air instead of bouncing off the walls. The walls were a blinding white with a maroon dome to top it off.

A line of stairs slithered around the cylinder like vines around a tree. Small suspension bridges connected the stairs to hanging islands clinging to the top dome by some pulley or chain or thick mooring rope. It was all so deftly rigged, so adequately spaced and engineered, that though there was cabling and wiring about the entire place, everything was neatly put, all excess order and coiled, and each space ornamented with odd-shaped slivers of glass giving off colorful reflections: it was a miniature city with strata over strata staged all the way aloft.

"Who are these people?" you asked.

"Iterations of me."

She took your bewilderment as her cue to explain.

"I could say I made them," she began, "I could say I *am* every single person in this lighthouse, which by the way there are many. For intents and their meanings, they were mass-produced, as if making pencils and putting them in a box, but they're not entirely the same. The differences are faint; there are slight distinctions that are all but negligible in your scheme of things, in your spectrum, but they are there.

"While pencils look identical in a box, they differ in what

art is made with them. Like people. *These* people. There are genetic diversities that arm each person with various capacities and inabilities, even if they are modeled after me. It is what they produce from their commonality which exalts them: art, science, philosophy – legacies for whose purpose people have created such an array of disciplines and fields of study and excellence. At this point, they've made so much out of that base commonality that I've got no claim to it anymore. At first I left them alone, until they got smart."

"How so?"

"Do you know when you make a copy of a document, and then you make another copy, you can tell it's a copy by the slight blank spaces in the letters?"

"Yes," you said.

"They noticed a similar discrepancy in their reality," she said. "They noticed a pallor, a tender misstep in their building blocks that felt almost holographic. When they looked at the very small – atoms, subatomic particles, etc. - they noticed a flicker. When they looked at the very large – planets, stars, and galaxies - the colors were a lot less vibrant than they should be given the numerical phenomena."

"So what did you do?"

"I told them the truth," she said. "I told them they were iterations of me. I told them I had created them."

"Didn't they get upset knowing they weren't real?"

"You know, they had the same reaction as you. They immediately labeled themselves as 'not real.' And it took me some time to understand why they thought that. What's the difference if a person made you or a so-called God did? Is it a need for association with a higher power? What if you're a product of Chance? Of Evolution, say. Initially, some of them liked the idea of being a product of Chaos. It meant they didn't owe anything to anyone, but I would argue they wouldn't owe it to a god, either. They certainly don't owe shit to me, and I did make them.

"But I made them for myself and my self-interest, to better understand myself, to see myself in all possible lights. They are no more than probable scenarios for me, simulations, if you will, through which I can study what my reactions and perceptions would be during various circumstances and environments. In short, they are hypothetical me's. So what do they owe me? Nothing. They didn't exist! If they did not exist, how could they possibly need anything? How can a thing that doesn't exist need to be saved? So, what favor was done here? Is existence objectively good even when it's unsolicited? They're a project. And they are excellent, yes, but they know why they're here, at least, and so far we've got on nicely."

She was reveling in your amazement, relishing in the contortions she knew your mind was making from the quivering of your face.

I didn't know she had been busy with all of that. Even I was amazed because though she may have sounded cynical to you, and borderline malicious, there was a tinge of good in her intentions.

No evil seeks to understand itself.

Evil exerts itself as the thing to be understood.

It is arrogant and petulant.

Evil asserts itself as the standard, the rule, and the law, the enforcer and creator of the norm.

In all its hubris, evil allows no space for change because acknowledging the need for growth admits insufficiency, and evil doesn't doubt itself.

"Look at her, for example," Iloveny said. "Leyla, could you come here, please?"

She was about fourteen. Her lush, auburn storm of a mane made her freckled face look as if it were on fire, about to be consumed, struggling to stay in view. She wore a white toga with a denim jacket over it. Converse shoes.

"Hello," you said.

"Ask her anything," Iloveny said. "Maybe she'll convince you."

You looked at her and asked, simply, "Where do you come from?"

"Where did I *come* from?" she laughed. "Do *you* even know that about yourself? Who cares! I'm here. Who made me? Who cares, I'm here. Why am I here? Who cares, I'm here. I know it may sound lazy to you, but it's liberating. Once I shrug off the absurdities of my existence – the Why's and How's and Who's – none of which I can control because they happened before I was a thing, I can focus on more important things."

"Like what?"

"Like where I'm going. Meaning, where I'm directing all the energy that is myself, and whether it is worth my while."

Iloveny tap your shoulder as if to release you from a trance.

"You should take look at the lighthouse," Iloveny said. "Go up the stairs. Take it all in. Leyla can show you around. Would you?"

"Gladly," Leyla said.

CHAPTER 52

What the fuck is going on? I asked myself inside your head. *What is all of this?*

And as I rummaged for some answers, Iloveny smiled.

"What have you done?" I asked her.

"I'm showing him his options," she said.

"I was going to tell him."

"When?"

"When he was ready!"

"That's what fear always tells itself."

"Fuck you."

***

I'll explain.

And I know you won't see this before she shows you.

Perhaps you'll never see it.

But I'll know I tried to tell you.

After death, and before birth, your soul is split into parts, fluttering around in what we've called the Collective Soul.

The Collective Soul is like a large lake where all your souls and permutations are kept and renewed. This, as a unit, is Humanity as an entity: a singularity to encompass all of your plurality. Your collected wisdom, knowledge, creativity, imagination – all of you into one.

After death, depending on how much a particular soul has grown, it retains its identity long enough to steep its spiritual achievements into the Collective Soul.

This is the case with those exalted spirits who, by improving themselves, have improved the species as a whole.

I need not give out names.

Still, even these heightened souls split into parts and return to their prime materials.

What makes *daemons* different is the absence of this splitting.

In your spectrum, the Collective Soul of a *daemon* would look like a wind-flattened lake of diaphanous waters, everything shining in ubiquity: everything equally spaced and excellently caged into a cyclical form of synchronous movement.

It was perfect.

But we can't study something that is perfect.

The only way to study it was by splitting it.

This what we did, and there was Iloveny and there was me.

But when we fell out, I chose to study things on my own, and for that I had to split things further.

Into me, and *you*.

This was my mistake.

And she loves the irony of it: the more we learned and discovered, instead of narrowing the mysteries we increased them, and the only omnipotence in the universe was the absurdity of it all, the baseless endlessness of a futile thought – hopeful at best – of ever being the entities we thought ourselves to be.

How I sometimes wish upon myself the bliss of ignorance.

What duty do we have to be supreme?

What compels us to 'be god'?

Nothing.

There's nothing I can do now.

She has you, and when she offers you to yourself, how could you possibly say no?

You were never real, Orlando, but maybe now you will.

CHAPTER 53

The stairwell was made with matted, wrought iron.

It had miniature busts scattered about the rails. The detail was meticulous. The style: Baroque. There were busts depicting philosophers from Thales of Miletus to Socrates, Plato, Zeno of Citium, Diogenes the Cynic, Epicurus – but it didn't follow a timeline, and I think that was the point… to show that wisdom is eternal, perhaps, and that its exponents shone like stars regardless of the time from which they shone, brightness is bright and full stop.

You also recognized Seneca, Musonius Rufus, Epictetus, Marcus Aurelius – you noticed the inclination toward the Stoics – Cicero was also there, in fact, and it went on to Lao Tzu, Confucius, Lao Tse, Siddhartha.

The busts went on and on until it all ended, right past Nietzsche and some others you couldn't recognize, with a familiar face: Goku.

You laughed.

"You're a *Dragon Ball* fan?" she asked.

"Huge one."

She smiled.

"That is the point I'm trying to make," she said. "What *is* the point of it all? A great sum of knowledge? Wisdom? A deep thought? What is the point for all our efforts if not Happiness?"

"And to you Happiness means – "

"Something simple," she said, "a flying joke, a feat of power, a touch of the supernatural, a flash of imagination, fast music, sweet language, heroic flair, filial madness, quirky faces – and to me, that simplicity is *Dragon Ball*."

CHAPTER 54

I'm so sorry.

I realized it too late.

I mean it, Orlando. I'm so sorry.

She distracted you, again, with everything you'd find stimulating. She goaded you with charm and caged you with a flash of intellect.

Who even speaks like that? Who the fuck is Leyla? A lighthouse of random people? Fancy wording? Goku?

She knew what she was doing. And I should've known better.

I'm sorry.

You are dead, Orlando.

You died the moment you entered the lighthouse.

And I didn't realize until now.

You're stuck there. Forever.

And *I'm* stuck here: in your body, lying on the ground until it rots.

And she is laughing because she won.

Once you leave the lighthouse you won't come back to this body.

You will go into another body, because I will be in yours, devolved into a mortal, and you will be an entirely new thing.

I'll tell you what she's done, and what she intends to do with everyone else:

You're a *daemon* now, Orlando.

And if it seems that your entire life all happened inside

your mind then, don't feel bad, because that's how it happens for everyone. You've just been made aware of it.

You've enjoyed reality beyond those who are so-called real.

And you were real to me.

Now you're a personality within another, like myself.

I didn't know this is how I came to be, nor will you, until you find this.

In time.

And whichever identity takes over the frame of your existence, I hope you can help as I hopefully helped you.

In a way, this is what you wanted...

Welcome to eternity, *lijo.*

The End.

ACKNOWLEDGEMENTS

I hope enough people read this so I can eventually fill this page with gratitude.

This work is all me.

No editor. No agent. No beta-readers.

I know it's a risk. And outright unadvisable. But things are hard and I can't afford any of the above.

Still, I'm grateful to all the people who kept me alive when I ate things off the floor, and all of those who have loved and hated me since.

Here it goes.

ABOUT THE AUTHOR

Orlando A. Rebolledo

Orlando A. Rebolledo graduated from the United States Merchant Marine Academy in 2014 with a BA in Marine Transportation and Logistics.

When he is not occupied playing with his daughter or getting lost in the woods, he works as a harbor pilot.

He lives in New Hampshire.